Schoolboy Johnson

BOOKS BY

John R. Tunis

Published by William Morrow & Company
HIS ENEMY, HIS FRIEND 1967
SILENCE OVER DUNKERQUE 1962
SCHOOLBOY JOHNSON 1958
BUDDY AND THE OLD PRO 1955
GO, TEAM, GO! 1954
YOUNG RAZZLE 1949
HIGHPOCKETS 1948
THE KID COMES BACK 1946

Published by Harcourt, Brace & Company
A CITY FOR LINCOLN 1945
ROOKIE OF THE YEAR 1944
YEA! WILDCATS! 1944
KEYSTONE KIDS 1943
ALL-AMERICAN 1942
WORLD SERIES 1941
CHAMPION'S CHOICE 1940
THE KID FROM TOMKINSVILLE 1940
THE DUKE DECIDES 1939
IRON DUKE 1938

JOHN R. TUNIS

Schoolboy Johnson

WILLIAM MORROW & COMPANY
New York

PUBLISHER'S NOTE: On baseball teams in the past, unlike those of today, it was not unusual for the team's manager to also play one of the positions in the field. In this book, Spike Russell is both the Dodgers' manager and its shortstop.

Printed in the United States of America.
HC 1 2 3 4 5 6 7 8 9 10
PA 1 2 3 4 5 6 7 8 9 10

Library of Congress Catalog Card number: 58-5728
ISBN: 0-688-10149-6
ISBN: 0-688-10150-X (pbk.)

CONTENTS

Schoolboy Johnson

CHAPTER 1

Old Timers' Day

Speedy Mason sat beside Dave Leonard in the Buick convertible driving slowly along the parkway. Once it had been a new, shining, impressive, and expensive automobile. Like the two men, old pals and teammates on the Dodgers, it was older now and looked it.

Dave was silent. He had been through it all, knew just how it felt; he had enough sense this late summer afternoon to keep quiet. What can you say to a man when a thing of this sort hits him? You can't say anything, so better not try. A man must live through it entirely alone.

Sooner or later, Speedy was thinking, this happens to everyone. It happened to Dave Leonard when Spike Russell took over the Dodgers, happened to Jocko Klein when that big Sunny Jim came along. Happened to Raz Nugent. Now it's happened to me! July the second, the day the sun stopped shining. The day I almost couldn't breathe.

This won't do at all, at all. Look here, Speedy, get aholt of yourself. This isn't the end of the world. Yet it is, in a way, because when baseball is your life, and it goes, a big slice of your world goes too.

It had to come some time, of course. He recalled vividly the brutal day when it came to the man at the wheel. And the afternoon it happened to Jocko Klein, who had done such a wonderful job in the World Series just the year before. Jake Stafford, the club secretary, had come shuffling past the bench that day, with everyone looking the other way.

Every man was thinking the same thing. Who, me? Not me! He doesn't mean me, does he?

All the while Jocko had sat there, staring off into center field, not saying a word, a dazed, kind of this-can't-happen-to-me expression on his face. And the gang busy with their bats, or going over to the water cooler, or rubbing rosin on their hands, pretending all the time not to notice. Everyone with that same uneasy question in his mind. Surely not me! But who's next?

So face up to it, big boy; this had to come. It comes to us all, some day. Didn't Harry Street shove Gabby Gus Spencer aside? Then later, Spike Russell came up from Nashville, and one afternoon, bang, Harry is playing second for Minneapolis. And what about me? When I went to the Giants, Phil Sundstrom was trying hard to hang on for another year, and I took the play away from him. Phil never hated me for it, and Jocko Klein didn't hate that Sunny Jim, either.

Yep, it had to come, only why couldn't they have waited until the season was over? Why did they have to do it on Old Timers' Day?

The man at the wheel patted his knee affectionately. "I realize how ya feel, Speedy. This kind of a knock needs a lot of getting used to—don't I know it!"

They drove along in silence. Dave Leonard knew; he understood.

But this apparent cruelty, this impersonal manner of tossing you out, is a part of baseball. Don't ever forget: baseball is a business. You don't like it? Go run a filling station. Nobody asked you to play baseball.

Of course he'd been sitting on the bench, he hadn't really pitched a lot lately; but what hurt was the way it happened. One minute he was on the field, joking and kidding, warm inside, full of happiness and laughter. Because this was Old Timers' Day, with a kind of celebration for all the Dodger veterans taking place before the regular scheduled game, and a lot of the old players were there: Jocko Klein and Raz Nugent; Elmer McCaffrey, the former southpaw; Harry Street and the rest. They were back again for a few brief moments to stand out on the diamond and be introduced to the crowd, many of whom had never seen them play, to listen to those cheers from the stands again. For a few minutes they were the Champs, not a lot of has-beens.

Then? Why, in the middle of that jollity and warmth—ice water. They told him MacManus wanted to see him.

The boss was in his office, behind the familiar desk, his manner blunt and impersonal as usual.

Brace yourself, feller, here it comes!

Words followed, words that meant nothing to Speedy Mason. Words about the necessity for bringing up a new reliefer, words about the waiver list and his being a free agent. All words, except one sentence that hurt so much it penetrated.

"You understand, don't ya, Speedy? You get paid to the end of the season. You're on your own, but you get paid to the end of the season."

Why, sure I get paid, sure I do. After all, there's a contract tucked away in that big safe of yours. Even you can't bust it; nobody can. And if the boys should happen to hit the Series, I'll get one share, maybe. More likely a half share or a quarter share. It's true I'm a free agent, but who wants a pitcher let out early in July by the Dodgers?

"No, Mr. Mac," he wanted to say. "No, it's something else, something you mightn't understand. Tomorrow another guy will have my locker, and a stranger will be wearing my old number. I won't be out there with the gang, warming up, or racing down to the bull pen. No, for the first time in years I'll be home, watching the game on television." That's what he wanted to say.

But Speedy Mason had said nothing. Instead he had turned and walked out of MacManus' office in silence and had gone down to the dressing room. He took off his uniform for the last time. Then he showered, cleaned out his locker, shook hands with the trainer and old Chiselbeak, the attendant.

"Sorry to see you go, Speedy. Sorry to see you leave."

He tried to get his home on the telephone, but the number was busy twice, and Dave Leonard was waiting, so they went up into the grandstand. It was a good ball game, with the Dodgers leading the Pirates 2-1, but neither man had any heart for it. After a few innings they both agreed they'd had it. Let's go.

All the way home Speedy kept thinking, I knew it was coming, of course I knew, how could I help knowing? I thought I was ready for the bad news any time, yet when it came I wasn't ready at all. Like Jocko Klein, who sat on the bench for a month watching that Sunny Jim burn up the league. Yet when the day actually came, Jocko looked as if he'd been hit by a Mack truck. Same way with me. I wasn't really ready for it either.

Well, I've saved a little dough. I got a few bucks in the bank. Perhaps I can land that broadcasting job in Kansas City. Only broadcasting isn't baseball. I don't want to *talk* a good game, I want to play. I'm a ballplayer's ballplayer; that's what Casey, the columnist on the *Mail*, always called me.

Why sure, I realize it was in the cards, it had to come, they haven't used me lately. I had to go down. But to do it on Old Timers' Day, after fifteen years in the majors and an earned-run average of .282 and almost 1400 strike-outs . . . that's what hurts!

Never again! I'll never again hear that yell when the announcer says, as I walk to the mound to start a game, "Pitching for Brooklyn . . . Speedy Mason . . . number 58."

"How's that, pal?" asked Dave Leonard, beside him, lighting a cigarette.

"Aw . . . nothing." Say, I surely am getting along when I begin mumbling to myself.

"Take it easy," Dave said. "A man needs time to get used to a thing like this. You'll get used to it all right."

"Yeah, Dave, guess you're right. You're dead right, Dave, old-timer." Yet in his heart he knew he was fooling himself. I'll never get over it, never. Once I was the second-best pitcher in the National League, Speedy Mason. . . . And watch that herky-jerky motion, watch yourself when you get aboard. Stay close to the bag. He's tricky.

Dave slowed down, turned off the parkway, drove through a suburban development, up a side street, down another, and stopped before a one-story house set back from the road.

"Mind you take it easy now, Speedy, take it easy. Make the missis fix you a good steak for dinner."

"Sure will. And thanks, Dave, for waiting for me, for bringing me out here, for staying alongside. You helped this afternoon; if it hadn't been for you, I'm certain I couldn't have taken it."

They shook hands. He shut the car door quietly and went up the walk toward the house, walking slowly as he had in the old days after a hard-fought game. When they lost, his wife always waited for him inside. She was inside now.

Hope she doesn't moan it up, he thought. I don't want that. It's bad enough, getting the old pink slip. After all, she knew it was coming, same's I did.

The second he entered the room and she came toward him, he knew she knew.

She kissed him. "Big boy, they sort of gave you the works today, didn't they?"

"Yep, this is one time I didn't duck. Still and all, it was coming sooner or later. I tried twice to get you on the phone; I wanted you to hear it from me. The line was busy both times."

"It's the wire services, the A.P. and the U.P. They've been calling all afternoon for a statement. I told them I didn't know when to expect you home. I heard it on television."

The screen door banged, and two boys roared into the room. "Daddy! Didja pitch today, didja?" asked the younger.

The older boy knew better. He simply asked, "Hey, Dad, did you get the ball? You didn't forget the ball for us, did you?"

Often after a long double-header or an extra-inning game, when he ached and was sore and weary inside and out, he hated to see the youngsters, to have to sit and explain what happened in the twelfth, or why he passed that man in the fourteenth. He wanted to be alone then, to forget the whole thing. Yet now he welcomed them; it was comforting to have them climbing all over him, took his mind off himself and his troubles.

He produced the ball from his pocket. "There you are, fellers, all the names of all the old-timers—Dave Leonard, Raz Nugent, Fat Stuff, they're all there."

They shared it together as he had taught them, not grabbing at it, but inspecting it together, rolling the ball over and over in their hands as they read the names with awe.

"See . . . Dave Leonard . . . Raz Nugent . . . Harry S. Street . . . Homer Slawson . . . Elmer McCaffrey. . . . They're all there, like he said."

"No, they're not. Where's Daddy's name?"

"Your name's not on it, Daddy. Aren't you an old-timer?"

He tossed his hat onto the davenport and stroked his thick black hair with the streaks of gray in it. "Nope, I'm not there. Those are the old-timers, not the men on the club nowadays. See, I'm not old enough to be an old-timer."

Nor young enough to be a Dodger, either.

CHAPTER 2

In the Minors

There had been a time when Speedy Mason couldn't sit in peace in a hotel lobby. The place might be entirely empty except for a couple of lounging bellhops; yet the moment he sat down, a figure would instantly appear at his elbow.

"Please, mister, please. Will ya. . . ."

The moment he settled into his chair, kids came to life by magic. They seemed to spring from the floor. Because, in every city, they knew where the ball clubs stayed, they recognized the players, and whenever they did not they merely asked everyone without a hat for his signature.

"Please, mister, please. . . ."

That afternoon the deserted, dingy lobby was devoid of human beings. No kids were to be seen. The fan clubs were ranging the lobby of the Commodore in New York, pestering the ballplayers seated against the marble columns of the Edgewater Beach Hotel in Chicago, and poking around the William Penn in Pittsburgh, sticking old score cards under players' noses, and asking, "Please, mister. . . ."

But nobody bothered you in a second-rate hotel in Savannah, Georgia, on a hot July afternoon. Speedy Mason, in the big leather chair, was left alone. He stretched out his legs and dozed, for he was tired. After pitching a hard night game in Columbia, the team had started for Savannah, and the bus got a flat. The spare was not reliable, so two rookies were told off to roll the injured tire five miles to the nearest town for a patch job. It was three hours before they started rolling again.

Now the remainder of daytime stretched endlessly ahead, hour after hour, until it was time to eat and go to the ball park. Speedy rose with a yawn and went over to the newsstand to get a paper and see what westerns were playing at the movie theaters. There had been a time when Speedy Mason tried to save his eyes during the baseball season. Now it didn't make much difference. Besides, as old Grouchy Devine, his manager when he was with the Giants, used to say, ballplayers who go to the movies seldom get into trouble.

He attempted to avoid the sports pages, with the Dodger box scores and the league standings, for all that was behind him, and he hated to be reminded of it. But before he reached the amusement section of the paper, a familiar name caught his eye.

New York, July 18. Roy Tucker, known as the Kid from Tomkinsville, who started with the Dodgers as a pitcher and played the rest of his career with them in center field, leading the National League three times in batting, was given his unconditional release today. His most notable achievement was hitting five home runs against the Yanks in the Series of. . . ."

So the Kid is through too! It really does happen to everyone, doesn't it? Let's see now; he's older than I am by quite a lot. He must be pushing forty. When I played with the Giants I used to hate the guy at times, there were so many ways he could beat you. Then later, on the same team with him, things were different. You realized how great a ballplayer he really was. A mighty good man to have on your side.

How many times I've faced him when I was pitching for the Giants, watched him stand there swinging his bat. A great guy when he had it, one of the best. He tried with everything he had, gave you nothing and asked for nothing. Now he's through too. It comes to us all.

A traveling salesman stepped from his car, and a bellhop went out to unload his bags. The front door slammed shut, but Speedy Mason wasn't watching. He was looking at a lean figure crouched over home plate, waving a tough-looking war club, and he was hearing the crack of a hard drive as the batter connected, and old Fat Stuff, the Dodger coach on first, shouted, "Go for two, Kid, go for two!"

Well, here I am sitting in a third-rate hotel in Savannah,

Georgia, and Roy Tucker is probably taking the train back to Tomkinsville, Connecticut, where he came from—finished, done with major-league baseball. If he doesn't like it he can always get a job in a bowling alley.

The newspaper slipped from his hands to the floor. He reached over for it, folded it, and stuffed it in the crack of the leather seat, behind his back. Right at that moment a red-hot poker game was going on in 318, but Speedy had no cash to lose. Kerry King, the manager, would be watching the Cincinnati game on television in his room; but Speedy felt a little sick of baseball just then. He rose, deciding to take in a western.

Ballplayers get used to hot weather, to the curtain of steam that hits you in Chicago in midsummer, to the terrible humidity from the Mississippi that hangs over St. Louis in August. But Savannah, he felt, was the worst yet. Until evening came, the heat of the Georgia summer overpowered him, defeated him, left him limp and exhausted. He stood, hesitating, unwilling to leave the air-conditioned lobby.

Suddenly he thought, Is it the heat, or is it me? I never used to mind the weather. Heat, cold, rain, snow—whatever the weather was, you took it as it came, along with your pay check, and never thought about it. Nowadays it's different. You watch thermometers, read the weather reports in the newspaper. You wake up each morning seeing the sunlight on the floor and thinking, Another hot one. Can I take it?

Why, last night, waiting in that bus for the tire to be fixed, I swear it was at least a hundred and fifteen.

Well, here goes! He went outside, where the heat smacked him in the face and dazed him. This is awful, he thought. I'm getting so I can't take it any more. I'm not an old-timer yet, but I'm too old for this minor-league grind.

"Hey, mister, please, mister, please. . . ."

A discouraged-looking youth in dungarees and a dirty sport shirt held out a pad and a pencil. Speedy hesitated. Then he recalled one of Raz Nugent's better remarks. "Glad to do it for you, son, glad to do it for you. When they stop asking old Raz for his autograph, that means I don't eat."

CHAPTER 3

Two Old Pals

The men seated together in the press box watched with wary and knowledgeable eyes. They had to be shown. Both knew that the test of a third baseman, of his skill, his reflexes, his anticipation, is the hard-hit ball down the line to the fielder's right. Once it gets through, the damage is done. Extra bases are the penalty.

This shot was a wicked smash toward the bag, one which surely looked headed for the fences. The runners on first and second were off and away.

"Wow! Looka that! Looka . . ." said one of the men in the press box.

From nowhere the player on the grass behind third charged over. He reached down and smothered the ball. It seemed to vanish, to die in his glove. He touched the bag for the force-out, then straightened up and made the long throw across the diamond.

The sparse crowd in the little ball park stood up, cheering. Roy Tucker's cap had fallen to the ground. He reached for it, crammed it down on his head, and came trotting in to the dugout. As they continued cheering, he touched his cap ever so slightly.

"Say! What a play! How's that for a play, Sid? He's old Sure Mitts, isn't he?"

"I'll say he is. The guy's a pro; he still has what it takes. Mighty few third basemen in the majors could have made that throw falling away as he did. Don't he stand out in this gang of patsies! Get McGreevy four more Tuckers, and he'll end up in the play-offs."

"Just so. Try and get 'em. Wonder why the Dodgers ever let him go?"

"He wasn't fast enough to play the outfield any more, they had him on the bench, and besides, he couldn't reach the fences the way he usta, either. A great guy when he had it, though."

"And still is. The best on this man's ball club, anyhow. By the way, I hear Speedy Mason won another tonight for Augusta."

"Doesn't surprise me. He's their whole team. And *there's* another old-timer with a lot left, too."

For Roy Tucker, just down from the Dodgers to the minors, things were hard to take. Perhaps the toughest of all were the long bus rides, often in the early-morning hours after a night game. Their conveyance was an old rattletrap that seldom had enough power, when loaded with players and their equipment, to make the hills. Consequently the driver would roar down grades at seventy or eighty, hoping to pick up enough speed to make the inclines. Usually they were halted by cops at least once a night, and avoiding a ticket, or worse, needed fast talking by the driver.

Roy had followed with interest the course of Speedy Mason before he himself had received his release, noticing that the former Dodger pitcher had spent a short time in the Montreal bull pen with no success, and then gone on down to Elmira. There, Roy assumed, he still was. But ten days later, observing a big six-footer warming up before their night game with Augusta, Roy's reaction was: "Why, that pitcher looks like old Speedy."

He stood tapping his bat against his heels, looked again, walked closer. Could it be? Same motion, same stance. Why, strike me dead, it's Speedy himself down here pitching for Augusta.

"Hey there, Speedy!"

The man stuck up one gloved paw, caught the ball from his receiver, and turned in his usual leisurely way. Though he could still move rapidly, Speedy Mason conserved his energy whenever possible.

"Hello there, Roy. I didn't know you were down here. Mighty glad to see you."

They shook hands. "Glad to see you again, Speedy. Yep, they sent me down soon after you left. How you makin' out?"

"Same's you. I have good days and bad ones. Get a regular pay check, though, and the family likes the idea. It's been tough going; had ptomaine poisoning in Montreal, and I never got straightened out until I hit Augusta. Some things stay with a man nowadays." He stood there, slapping the ball from hand to hand in that familiar nervous gesture.

"Don't they, though, Speedy. How you feeling now?"

"Fine since I started pitching regular. I got to pitch in rotation. Say, I'm hitting, too; came up the other night and got me a triple. Like to die a-laughing out there on third. Well, Roy, what say we get together and have some chow after the game? I know a joint that stays open all night."

"Right." Roy moved away, watching Speedy Mason turn and toss the ball in to his catcher. There's a ballplayer for you, he thought. That man don't discourage easy.

He had plenty of chances to get discouraged that night. In the second, two outfielders let an easy pop fly drop between them as they stood watching. The first baseman twice messed up throws, the shortstop allowed a grounder to go between his legs, and every inning there were men on bases. The pitcher was under a continual strain; but he managed, pretty much on his own, to keep men from scoring.

An hour later Roy Tucker walked back from the plate to the bench, swinging his bat in disgust. "Shucks, they told me Speedy Mason had lost the hop on his fast one, but he's as fast as ever. Got that control, too; he still puts the ball exactly where he wants it."

"Relax, boy," said McGreevy, the manager. "You ain't the only one gone down swinging tonight. Our boys act like it was against the law to get a base hit. This weather will catch up with him, though; he can't take the heat, he won't last. We'll get to him."

But they didn't get to him. In fact, as the game went on, Speedy seemed to get better. Despite his wretched support, he hung on, and if the heat bothered him he showed no signs of it. Both teams were helpless at the plate, and nobody scored as they went into the ninth, the tenth, and the eleventh. Finally, in the twelfth, after getting the first batter, Speedy passed a man.

Roy Tucker stepped up to the plate with a man on second and one out. On the mound, the big fellow with the dark, unshaven cheeks glared down. Once that sight had terrified every batter in the National League. Tonight as he stood there, looking into his catcher's mitt and slapping the ball from hand to glove, he was as formidable as ever.

The two men had been enemies on opposing clubs, then teammates. Now they were enemies again. As Roy swung his bat, he knew Speedy Mason would bear down extra hard. The pitcher stepped off the mound and leaned over the rosin bag, making him wait. He stood rubbing the ball in the palms of his hands, as if to make it smaller.

Instantly Roy backed from the box and, leaning over,

scooped up dirt with his hands. No, sir, that's an old trick of Speedy Mason's; he makes me wait, I'll make him wait. So he wiped dirt carefully up and down the handle of the bat and, stepping in, noticed the sweat stains under the pitcher's arms, all over his uniform. He saw the deep lines of fatigue about his mouth.

Is he tired! I'm a lot older than he is and I'm tired too, but he's been throwing twelve innings of tough baseball.

So he stepped in confidently. Speedy often wasted his first pitch, throwing close in hopes of catching a man digging in with his spikes. He knows I remember this, so most likely he'll try to cross me up by doing that very thing. Well, I'm ready.

As he anticipated, the ball was on his fists. Roy leaned back and laced it over second. It was a well-hit blow, but straight at the center fielder's mitt, so the runner off second darted back to the bag.

The ball soared out, into the fielder's hands . . . and bounced out as if it had struck rubber. Instantly the runner on second roared into third as the fielder scrambled for the ball and started to throw. The runner kept on without stopping, and the fielder let go with a heave that was ten feet off home plate. The runner scored and the game was over.

On the mound, Speedy stood motionless. His head moved ever so slightly from side to side. Three hits and a base on balls, and you lose it in the twelfth because a clown who should be selling popcorn in a movie theater can't handle a simple line drive right in his fists. How good does a man have to be to win?

But Speedy showed no annoyance. Instead, he removed his cap, wiping his forehead with his sleeve. No angry remark to the fielder who hustled past him, no signs of temper or pique. He simply turned and walked slowly toward the dugout, stuffing his glove into his pocket as he went.

Roy knew exactly how he felt. The man was finished. He had given everything in those last innings, and nothing was left; he was drained, empty. Yet how different from most ballplayers, from most pitchers, who slump off the mound after a losing game, heads down, shoulders sagging. Speedy stalked away with pride, his bearing affirming his attitude.

Look, he seemed to say. Look, I've still got it! Three hits in twelve innings. I'm still Speedy Mason. Except for that clown out there in center field. . . .

Speedy Mason was another breed of cat, different from the ordinary pitcher, different even from Raz Nugent. Raz had been a twenty-five-game winner, a top-class hurler with an ego like a porcupine's. This man is a class guy. He's a great human being. He has character.

I wish he was on my side.

CHAPTER 4

A Call for Help

Baseball managers are as different from each other as the Marx Brothers. They have only one thing in common: an enormous desire to win. Nuff Sed McGreevy was like the rest in this respect. He was a compact, emphatic little man, as broad as he was tall, who owned a tavern in Chicago over which he presided in winter. Whenever disputes arose and voices grew taut, McGreevy would stalk around the bar, tap the client gently on the shoulder, and utter two words: " 'Nough said."

If the customer still remained boisterous and unpleasant, he would suddenly find himself out on Indiana Avenue, bouncing off the fenders of the cars parked before the tavern. Hence the manager's name, Nuff Sed.

Ten days later, when the two teams were due to meet again, Roy picked up Speedy in the afternoon to take in a movie. From the usual mixture of kids coming up, players good enough for the minors who would never get any farther, and a sprinkling of veterans on the way down-hill, Roy turned to him as a friend whenever the chance arose. Though they were on different teams, they were living through the same hard experience together, and Roy felt as close to Speedy Mason now as he had ever felt to anyone on the Dodgers.

Late that afternoon when they left the movies, a sharp, shrill whistle came from across the street. "Hey there! Roy Tucker, hey Roy!" One of the boys on the team was calling. "McGreevy wants you. He's been looking for you all afternoon."

They hurried to the little hotel and were met by an-other teammate. "Say, Tucker, Nuff Sed is after you. He's been ringing your room every twenty minutes."

The two men looked at each other, wondering what this could mean. Nowadays whatever happened to either of them seemed to be unfortunate; consequently their faces were serious as they went into the lobby.

Speedy said, "I'll buy a paper and wait for you here. Come down and break it to me easy, Roy."

Roy took the elevator to the third floor. Is this another step down, he wondered, as he walked along the corridor, or am I being asked to manage some tank-town team in the Three-Eye League? Whatever it is, it won't be good news. The poker game was on as usual in 318; the slap-slap of cards and the calls of the players came through the open transom. McGreevy's front room was the only air-conditioned one on the floor, and the cool draft was a relief to Roy after he had knocked and entered in response to the manager's grunt.

Nuff Sed was in a big chair, talking into the telephone. He motioned to another chair and continued. "Well then, Sam, see what you can do. I say, see what you can dig up for me. Losing my third baseman a few weeks before the end of the season this-a-way. . . . Yeah, it's always the same; we're the poor relations, we don't count. I got a club of bat boys and coaches. All right, I'll hear tomorrow then, Sam." He stopped and looked up, staring, one hand still on the phone.

Now then, thought Roy, let's have it. Gimme the bad news; don't wait, McGreevy, I can take it.

"Where in the blazes have you been all afternoon, Tucker—out at that golf club?"

"Why no, boss, Speedy and I were at a western."

"That's right, ruin your eyesight—what you old-timers got left. Roy, I have news. You're for the Dodgers."

"The Dodgers?" If the manager had said he was due to fly to the North Pole that evening, Roy would have been less astonished.

"That's right, this accident to Martin."

"Accident? What accident?"

McGreevy looked at him quickly. "Good grief, feller, don't you ever read the sports pages? Ray Martin, Dodger third baseman, broke a leg sliding into second at Chicago yesterday. They want you right away to fill in."

"At third? But look, McGreevy, I'm no third baseman."

"You're not, hey? What you been doing these past weeks out there—playing croquet? Russell called this morning to ask were you doing a job. What else could I say: of course he's doing a job, he's making plays no one else in this league can. You're a third baseman; I say you're a third baseman. O.K., you're a third baseman. The plane leaves the airport at seven, the bus will come at six-thirty, and Jerry has your ticket. Yes, and then where does that leave McGreevy? With a rookie on third and my best infielder gone. Not that you care—or Spike Russell either."

Roy Tucker could hardly speak. He was dizzy. As they shook hands, he realized that sometimes good news, like bad news, takes a lot of getting used to. He went down in the elevator, dazed and uncertain.

Speedy was smoking a cigarette and reading the evening paper. He stuck out his fist when he heard the news. "Say, this is great stuff. I'm sure glad for you, Roy; I'm mighty happy. What a chance you got!"

"Yeah, but at third base. . . . I'm an outfielder, not an infielder."

"They have to use you; they got no choice. It's either you or a utility man like Cross, who bats .242 or less."

"Well, maybe, I dunno. I never played third but once until I came down here last month."

"Wouldn't say you done too badly. McGreevy hasn't

kicked, has he? Way you been handling the base lately, you needn't worry."

"So it's the Dodgers again, and the hot corner this time." He was trying to accustom himself to this change of fortune.

"The hot corner! As old Grouchy Devine, my manager on the Giants, used to say: 'What's hot about it? Feller stands in the shade all afternoon and handles two, maybe three chances.' "

"Yes, sure, I know and all . . . only they gave me an unconditional release just last month."

"So what? You were a free agent, you hooked on down here, now they need you bad. Lucky for you that some last-place big-league club didn't have sense enough to grab you off in July; you'd never be on third base against the Yanks in October, way you will now. And maybe I don't envy you." He flipped away the cigarette and leaned toward the man sitting in the other cracked leather chair. "Tell ya another thing, Roy. That club needs a reliable pinch hitter. To pinch hit, you've got to be an old-timer; they don't develop pinch hitters down here in the minors, believe me. Well, looks like you better get upstairs and pack. I'll come along and help."

They took the elevator and went up to the dingy room. On two chairs beside the windows were two suitcases—open. Roy Tucker always lived out of his suitcases, believing that if you never put clothes in bureau drawers, you never left town forgetting anything.

A toothpick in his mouth, Speedy Mason sat on the bed, watching. There was pleasure in his gaze and a little envy in his heart. "Roy, do something for me; do me a favor up there, will ya?"

"Betcha life, Speedy, what is it?"

"Gimme a build-up with Spike Russell." The words came out suddenly; the voice was strained.

Roy had been leaning over his suitcases; now he straightened up.

Speedy Mason's face was intense, his eyes eager. Desire, hope, anxiety were all apparent. I'm back to the big tent, thought Roy, and Speedy is staying with Augusta, with this crowd of third-raters. He must feel terrible. No wonder he wants to get away from here and get back up there.

"If I pitch regular, if I throw in rotation, I can be of use to him now. My back's good. You saw; it lasted twelve innings the other night. I was still going strong at the end; you faced me, you watched me pitch. What was it, three hits in twelve innings? That ain't so bad, even for the Sally League. Speak to Russell; be a good guy. I can help if I pitch regular, I'm no gamble, I still got it, Roy."

"I'll say you got it, Speedy. You bet you got it—I ought to know, I hit against you. Sure I'll speak to Russell; of course I will, depend upon it."

"Just a chance, gimme one chance, that's all I need. Pitch me regular and he can't lose. I got no chance in Montreal, then I was sitting on the bench all the time I was in Elmira. I have to pitch in rotation or my arm stiffens. But give me an assignment every four days, and I'll beat anyone in the National League over nine innings."

All the strength, all the fortitude of the man, vanished. This proud veteran was begging. Roy had never seen him like this. He was desperate now, throwing away his pride just as he tossed four wide ones to a dangerous hitter. Here in this dingy bedroom, unseen by anyone except a pal, he was just an old ballplayer asking for another crack at it. This tough, hard competitor, who never gave or asked for anything, was pleading for one more chance in the big time.

Roy was rocked. He realized how his own good fortune had hit the man, and saw the struggle going on inside him.

Speedy rose, came over, and put one hand on his shoulder. "You'll speak to Spike, you'll tell him, tell him the facts, just say I've still got it, won't you? Won't you, feller?"

"I'll do better'n that. Man who can really do you good is Fat Stuff, the pitching coach. He was a veteran when I came up from Nashville as a pitcher, then he was first-base coach, now he handles the hurlers."

Mason frowned. "Oh . . . Fat Stuff. Yeah, that's different; y'see, Fat Stuff don't care too much for me. Fact is, we usta throw at each other's noggins in the old days when I played for the Giants."

"But you and he always got on all right when you were in the same club. Fat Stuff won't remember those old times; he's only interested in one thing—his pitching staff. It's shot now; that's why they need you, Speedy. I'll work on old Fat Stuff and let him do the selling on Russell. That's the best way to handle it. 'Course now, if Spike asks me, I'll give it back to him as straight as I can. 'Why, Spike,' I'll tell him, 'you'd be real lucky to grab him off before someone else does.' "

"Not as a reliefer, remember, not in the bull pen—don't forget that. I'd hate to say no—I want to get back the worst way—but I won't come up to sit out there and pitch a few innings a week."

This far and no more, his pride seemed to be saying. He knew his abilities and his weaknesses; he was wise enough to realize what he could and what he couldn't do. He rose from the bed again and looked out of the dingy window as Roy shut one suitcase.

"Tell ya what, Roy. I've been shuffled around considerable, but nobody ever teed off on me yet. It's not a question of age. I'm a lot younger than a good many pitchers in the majors right now, than Krebs of Cincinnati, or Green of the Cubs, or Morgan of the Cards. I've been round a good many years, that's true; but the point is I started young. And it's the shape you're in that really counts. I still got it; I'm smarter than these kids. Just so I get regular work, understand?"

He walked nervously back and forth. Roy could see

how much this faint hope of getting back meant to him. The telephone jangled. Speedy picked it up. "Yeah? No, but he's right here. O.K. He'll be down in just a minute." He replaced the phone. "The cab is down there waiting, and then the plane, and tonight you'll be up there. Well, this is good-by, feller. Whatever happens, I wish you luck. All the luck in the world. Speedy Mason will be pulling for you."

CHAPTER 5

Schoolboy Johnson

"You'll want mebbe yer same number, Kid."

Chisel handed over his uniform. Chiselbeak had been with the club when Roy Tucker came up as a rookie before the war. He was on hand when Roy returned from France. And here he was, apparently ageless, still shuffling around, his arms full of wet, sweaty clothes. Chisel had seen them come and go; he preferred the old-timers. To him Roy was a friend he always addressed as Kid.

The clean shirt with the big 34 on it fell across Roy's lap. He fingered it. This piece of flannel was only the upper part of a baseball uniform: the most uncomfortable costume ever devised by man, except a suit of armor. That afternoon it seemed the most beautiful thing in the world.

"Yeah, Chisel, thanks, Chisel. Mighty kind of you to remember."

Now, how's that for you? Chisel understands ballplayers; he knows what makes a man tick. Instead of handing over my locker to Jackson Jones and giving my number to one of the kids, like this Schoolboy Johnson, he saved it for me.

There, spread across his knees, was the uniform: number 34.

He removed his clothes slowly, looking around the high-ceilinged room, seeing the familiar sight of men in various stages of undress, hearing the same voices and the same noises, smelling the odor of ointments from Doc's room at the end. Being away a month had given him a clear, sharp picture of the team he knew so well and had served so long. He thought back to his first time up, way back when he was the Kid from Tomkinsville and his salary was so small he was glad to get an extra five dollars for helping Chisel with the bats.

Many of the older men had disappeared, even some he had watched push up to the majors, including a few by whose side he had fought through to five pennants. Dave Leonard was a successful contractor in Sarasota, Florida. Raz Nugent was managing a bowling alley in Fresno, California, showing his clippings around. Harry Street ran a filling station in Erie, Pennsylvania. Jocko Klein was doing a job as manager of Birmingham, in the Southern Association. Homer Slawson was gone, Jim McCaffrey was gone, Bonesy Hathaway was gone. Only a few of the veterans were left.

Red Allen had slowed up but was still busting fences all over the league. Karl Case remained in right, his throwing arm not so sharp, his speed on the bases diminished. Bobby Russell frisked around second as usual, and Highpockets ranged far and wide in left. Spike Russell, furrows on his brow and gray around the ears, was almost an old-timer manager now.

Most of the newcomers were colored guys: Sunny Jim, the short, roly-poly catcher; Jackson Jones, who had edged Roy out of the center-field slot; Ed Peters, the brilliant shortstop; big Josh Crayton, the dependable pitcher.

Schoolboy Johnson was a newcomer too.

Johnson, hey? Fans always spoke of him with a question mark. Say, what about this young Johnson?

Schoolboy Johnson, up from the minors, was the season's enigma. Every club had wanted him; every club had tried to get him. The Dodgers latched on to his contract early, and what they paid in dollars they never cared to disclose.

Roy watched him with interest as he warmed up. This guy doesn't know it, but he gave me some bad moments. It was to make room for Schoolboy Johnson they sent me down to the South Atlantic League. So he looked him over with attention.

The boy was a natural, a six-foot-two Californian with everything: speed, power, control. Once he ran the 100 in 9.5 for U.C.L.A. He could hit with the best. In the box he figured to be the Dodgers' big winner, the stopper of the pitching staff—which they badly needed. Yet in his few weeks in the majors he had won only a couple of games.

As the infield tossed the ball around while the umpires were taking the batting orders at the plate, Roy observed him carefully. The big chap was loose, graceful, easy of movement, with the makings of a real pitcher.

Then came the voice of the announcer, calling their names, until he got to: ". . . and on third base . . . Roy Tucker . . . number 34. . . ."

A roar swept the field. It drowned out the next names. He could hear the fans calling at him with affection from the stands. Kicking the dirt nervously behind third, he waved his arms in circles, pulled at his shirt slightly to free his armpits, thinking, It's sure good to be back. It's great to be back and in the middle of it again.

The first notes of The Star-Spangled Banner turned everyone toward the flagpole in center. Roy saw the boy standing beside the rubber remove his cap, observed the mane of thick blond hair. The pitcher seemed all youth, and Roy envied him. Good grief, how I must look beside these youngsters. The Dodgers have an old man on third base!

They were playing the Redlegs, who were in first place by two games, at the start of an important series. Spike had called Roy back to bolster a sagging infield. That afternoon the manager was tossing in his star pitcher to take the opener, for everyone knew Cincinnati was one of the teams to beat.

At the moment, second place was an uneasy spot. Two games behind the Dodgers were the Braves, with the fourth-place club scrambling at their heels. Somehow, the Dodgers, this team with too many players beyond their prime, had struggled along all season to stay up front, winning with a stubborn belief in themselves and their skills. Now, nearing the last month of the season, pride was not enough. They had to produce or go under.

That afternoon Schoolboy Johnson was hot. The Cincinnati sluggers were in his hand. He threw with a lusty recklessness as if daring them to hit, burning the ball past the best of them. By bunting and sacrificing, by flies deep to the outfield, the Dodgers had managed to get a lead of two runs going into the eighth inning.

The first Redleg batter in the eighth worked a full count and stood fouling off pitches, balls that might or might not catch the corners, the dangerous ones to let go by. He's doing this on purpose, thought Roy, he's working on this boy, trying to wear him down if he can. That's smart baseball.

But finally a pitch was low and the man walked. Immediately, action started out in the bull pen.

Bobby Russell, behind the box, took the ball from Sunny Jim and walked in to hand it to the Schoolboy. "Only six men, kid, just six left; leave us go get 'em."

The first pitch was a called strike. Then Johnson, after looking over his shoulder at first, burned in another. It was a ball. Next came a second ball, close but high. The pitcher shook his head and stood there, protesting. Immediately the catcher and most of the infield surrounded him. They seemed to expect this outburst, and they hung around him while he cooled off.

His next was carefully aimed, a beauty down the middle. The batter instantly stepped forward and laid a finely clipped bunt along the first-base line that died halfway to the bag. Retreating toward third, Roy observed the Schoolboy storm in as Bob Russell covered first.

Watch it, boy, watch it, don't be in a hurry. Take your time, plenty of time, feller. . . .

The pitcher grabbed at it, fumbled the ball a second, turned, and fired it into right field.

Then came the familiar pattern. The whole diamond was in motion, the runners eating up the paths, the fielders scrambling for the various bases. Yet there was a difference. Instantly Roy realized they were running on Karl Case. In the old days nobody took chances with that arm.

The lead runner came into third and the batter slid under the tag at second. On the mound, Schoolboy Johnson slapped the ball nervously from one hand to the other. He poised on the slab, glanced with wrath at the men on bases, shook off his catcher, nodded, and with no windup, threw.

Bang! A perfect line drive over second bounced away from Jackson Jones and both men came across to tie the score.

Slowly Spike Russell walked to the mound. The brain trust—Sunny Jim, the catcher; and the two veterans, Red Allen and Bob Russell—gathered around. Roy saw the pitcher's head nod with emphasis. He wanted to stay in. The group broke up; Spike recrossed the base path, returned to the dugout, and the game continued.

The first pitch was out of control, half stopped by the catcher. It bounced high in the air and fell behind the plate. Before Sunny Jim recovered it, the runner was standing on second.

Roy slapped his glove. "O.K., big boy, just let him smell it. Let him smell it, then take it away again." His tones were confident but he felt uneasy.

This lad doesn't look just right to me. A few minutes ago he was standing them on their ears; now he hasn't got it. What happened?

The rest of the infield was worried also. Bob Russell pawed the ground nervously, making stabs at breaking for second. Peters, at short, tugged the peak of his cap. Red Allen leaned over and tossed a couple of pebbles into the air.

"Strike one."

Wow, what a fast ball! The batter never saw it. Roy had never seen a man throw harder than this Johnson. When he was good, he was really good.

"Strike two."

The crowd yelled as he went ahead of the hitter, a slugger and bad man in the clutches, who stood waving his bat with a threatening gesture.

The Schoolboy wasted one, then burned in his fast ball again, his money pitch. But this time the batter was ready.

He met it. In a great arc, rising, rising, the ball soared high over the center fielder into the bleachers.

Spike didn't bother to come out. From the step of the dugout he waved insistently toward the Dodger bull pen.

Johnson watched. With a petulant gesture he tossed his glove into the air. It fell not too far from Roy, astride third, while the runners rounded the bags to make the score 4-2. The young pitcher stalked closer, his face black with rage, his composure gone, all poise abandoned. When he reached the place where the glove lay, he drew back and gave it a vicious kick. The glove arched into the air, sailed up, and dropped almost on the concrete steps of the dugout.

The shouts that had greeted the homer died away. Everyone was concentrating upon the pitcher. A strange, unpleasant silence fell over the ball park.

Roy stared with the rest. Say, if this is Spike's best chucker, he may not be too hard to sell on old Speedy Mason.

CHAPTER 6

Manager's Conference

The youngsters want to be with the winners. They follow the latest, most successful band leader, the best sweet singer, and the championship ball club. They chase name band leaders for signatures, they know exactly where the baseball players stay in every city, when they come and where they go.

But that night the station was lonely and deserted. The vast, blue vaulted roof made it a kind of huge hall of silence; the few travelers boarding trains walked quietly, talked in low tones as they went across to the Pullmans. At last, one by one or in pairs, the team began to arrive.

Jerry Sands, the club secretary, was standing at the gate checking off names as they went past. With them came the youngsters. From every side they seemed to spring from the floor, knowing which gate the train left from, the time it departed, and how the players often went in by an opened grill beyond the big lighted sign that flashed the name of the train and the stations.

TRACK 26

Southwestern Express

Buffalo
Cleveland
Cincinnati
Indianapolis
St. Louis

The kids wore dirty dungarees, loafers, and bobby socks. As one player after another appeared, the crowd grew: Spike with Fat Stuff, Jackson Jones sloping along with Ed Peters, Karl Case and the tall, angular High-pockets, squat Sunny Jim Carter, and the man in the battered straw hat. Roy was the only one of the lot to wear a hat. Once the kids would have mobbed him. Now he passed by unnoticed. For they were after the stars of the club, the names: Schoolboy Johnson and Sunny Jim, the home-run king. They follow the names and ignore the losers.

"Please, mister, will ya . . . please. . . ."

The club was loose and free as they boarded the South-western. For they had come back to take the next two games from Cincinnati, and were only one out of first. We got 'em. We're the champs, we enjoy this kind of a rat race, we'll catch 'em because they have butterflies in their throats and butterfingers attached to their arms. We're tough, we're used to every game being the big one, the one that counts.

Winners travel in style, and they shoved their stuff into the roomettes, ranged up and down the aisle.

"Hey, Roy, you chow yet?" said Fat Stuff, passing by the open door of Roy's roomette. He leaned against the panel, looking inside.

"Not yet. I'm really tired tonight; I don't eat right after a game any more when I feel bushed like this. Can't handle the grub. Come in, sit down a minute."

It seemed the moment for which he had been hoping, the big chance to get the old pitching coach alone and mention Speedy Mason. So he got up, ready to shut the door, beckoning his teammate inside.

But to his surprise the old fellow shook his head. "Come on down to the boss's compartment. He wants to see you."

Now what, thought Roy, as they moved down the aisle to the other end of the car, where Spike Russell was sitting in a big chair, dressed in red-and-white striped pajamas, glancing at an evening newspaper. Red Allen, in a sport shirt, was on the couch.

The manager looked up, saw them in the doorway, tossed the paper to the floor. "Come in, Roy, come in, fellers. That Casey, he's quite a character—so he thinks. Any angle for a story, anything for a story, hey! Shut the door, Fat Stuff. You guys are gonna chow in here with me."

Roy removed his coat, tossed it onto the rack above, opened the collar of his shirt, shook off his shoes. This is quite a lot different from the Sally League, he thought. Just about this time Speedy Mason and McGreevy and the rest of that gang are whizzing down hills chased by a Georgia cop in a prowl car. The temperature is 106, it's just cooled off, and the boys are dead-beat after a long game. No thanks, thought Roy. This is the way to travel.

"There, by golly, that's better, that's better."

The game had wearied him, but in the cooling air of the gently moving Pullman he felt better. For he perceived he was being asked to a meeting of the older heads on the club. There were situations to be cleared up, and one Roy had to clear up, also.

But just how could he bring up Speedy's name? It would have been much easier if he had cornered Fat Stuff alone in his roomette, or had the Skipper to himself.

They sat silent for a few minutes, like workmen who have done a commendable job and earned a little respite from their labors. They spoke infrequently, thinking of that game lost yet finally won. That's why we're the champs. Then Spike shook his head.

"The pitching! The pitching—that's what really has me down."

Why, here it is in my lap, thought Roy, glancing out the window across the Hudson and at the electric signs flashing on the Palisades. Spike brought it up; I didn't. He's taken the first and hardest step for me. After all, the direct way is the best way. I'll simply let him have it.

"Your pitching's rough, Spike."

"Three in there yesterday, four pitchers today. Seven in two days. How in the world we ever win ball games, I dunno," remarked Fat Stuff solemnly.

Red Allen had nothing to offer, but Roy knew he was thinking the same thing they all were. Except for the hitting and the fielding—especially the hitting—we'd be in sixth place and no doubt about it.

Roy persisted. "Skip, you need a steady, reliable starter."

"I need a good reliefer, a reliable starter, a left-hander who can throw; correction, I need a pitching staff."

"Just an idea, Spike; forget it if it's out of order." He hesitated. Is this the right moment, before these other men? Or should I wait to go through Fat Stuff? Nope, Fat Stuff and Speedy never did take too kindly to each other. Besides, everything comes to him who doesn't wait. This is my chance, it's Speedy Mason's chance; I'll grab it. Here goes!

"Let's have it, Roy; you been round a long time, you know pitching. Got any suggestions?"

"Why yes, I have. Ever thought of Speedy Mason?"

Fat Stuff looked up, a frown on his face. Red Allen slapped his thigh and grunted. "There's one old-timer who's a fighter every minute."

For a while nobody spoke.

"Roy," said the manager, "mebbe you got something there. With a guy like Speedy out in the bull pen. . . ."

"No."

"No? Why not?"

"Because. Just plain no."

"I don't getcha, Roy. No what?"

"I mean no, just no, no bull pen. No soap, he won't bite."

"Ha, he won't bite, you say he won't bite. Speedy's up fifteen, eighteen years; now he's down with some tank town in Georgia. Try to tell me he won't go for a share of that Series dough."

"Just so, Fat Stuff, that's what I'm saying. He will *not* come back to sit in the bull pen, even a Dodger bull pen. He needs to pitch regularly."

"Now wait a minute, Roy; this doesn't sound reasonable. An old-timer like Speedy would jump to get back into the majors."

"You don't know Speedy Mason as well as you think, Fat Stuff. He has to pitch in rotation or his arm stiffens. Throw him in there every four or five days and he'll win six or seven games between now and October. Way things are going, that could mean the pennant, Spike; but nothing doing in that bull pen, I'm telling you."

"Hold on. His arm tightens, hey?" Fat Stuff spoke reflectively.

"Sure; his arm tightens if he has to sit out there in that

bull pen. Not if he gets regular work. I played against him down there, I know what I'm saying—he's a different man. And nothing upsets him, nothing. Guys kick the ball around, they mess up vital plays, he's always the same, steady, reliable. Never blows his top—and by golly, we sure had an exhibition of a man blowing his top today. 'Course, Speedy hasn't the fast ball he once had, nor he hasn't Schoolboy's temper, either, blowing up like that."

Fat Stuff broke in. "H'm. I never did like Speedy. I always hated the guy's guts when he was on the Giants, a doggone mean *hombre* for my book. Usta throw at my head."

Roy was ready. "Sure, and you threw at his."

The old pitcher replied in a shocked tone, as if he had been accused of murder. "Oh, no, Roy, I never threw at his head, never. 'Course now, I may've shoved him back from the plate a little; you boys all remember Speedy liked to dig in up there. Any hitter does that got to expect a few tight ones."

"Never mind all that, Fat Stuff," Spike said. "Sell that to Casey or some other sports writer. I'm interested in him as a pitcher; you like him, you don't like him, it's all the same to me. Roy, how's he been doing this past month?"

"Great, simply great. He wins, he loses, but he's with one of the all-time worst teams of baseball, and he's chucking like Bob Feller. I've seen him give up three hits in twelve innings and lose the game. His support would break the back of an elephant. He's six and three, I believe. Put a ball club like this one behind him, he'd really be something."

"Yeah," interjected Red Allen, "he's so darn good, why'n Montreal hang onto him? Tell me that. He was no use at all in Montreal, no use at all."

Roy turned on the big first baseman. "Two reasons. One is he got ptomaine poisoning up there and was sick most of the time. 'Nother is, they kept him in the bull pen. I'm telling you all, give him a chance to do his stuff regularly, and he'll win plenty for you. I'll guarantee it."

The manager looked at the pitching coach, the coach looked at the manager, and they both glanced at Red. The train was rocking along beside the Hudson. Up ahead was a huge bridge clogged with lighted cars. They sat peering out the window. Then they returned to baseball, to the situation their club faced, to an old-timer sweating in an un-airconditioned bus somewhere on U. S. 80 outside Macon, Georgia.

"He might help with that young fireball," Spike said thoughtfully.

Roy was mystified. What did Speedy Mason and pitching in rotation have to do with that crazy maverick?

There was a knock at the door. "You gentlemen want menus?" said the porter. He handed out four cards as large as flying saucers.

"Yes, we'll order. But first off, porter, I want a telegraph blank. Can we send a wire from Harmon?"

"Certainly, sir; train stops at Harmon ten minutes."

"Good. Get me a coupla blanks. What's the address, Roy? Augusta Baseball Club, Augusta, Georgia?"

CHAPTER 7

Speedy's Return

Ball players come and go like the seasons. A youngster in Texas gets a wire that his contract has been switched from a Class B farm club to the Double A's. He is on the long road up.

A man of thirty-two is sitting on the bench in Kansas City when the club secretary beckons and breaks the news that he is now the property of Indianapolis. He's started on the short slide down.

A veteran of eighteen years in the big time is standing beside the upraised hood of an ancient bus in front of a ball park in Columbia, South Carolina, watching the driver change a worn-out fan belt. Someone hands him a wire ordering him to report to the Dodgers in St. Louis as soon as possible. He's been up, come down; now he's on the way back once more.

The club was suiting up in the locker room in Busch Stadium in St. Louis when Speedy Mason arrived. Chiselbeak, the locker attendant, one foot on a chair, was talking in a corner to Casey of the *Mail*.

Chisel knew them all, better than anybody, better even than Spike Russell, the manager, whose real business was not baseball but the study of mankind. The old fellow saw them in their nakedness, in their moments of joy and sorrow, in their sadness after defeat and their gladness after victory, when they were bushed, exhausted, beaten— or delirious with joy. At a time when no pretences prevailed, when their defenses were shattered. When for good or bad these men were really themselves.

The locker man and the sports writer watched the gang surround Speedy Mason that evening, clapping him on the back and pumping his hand. A few newcomers like the Schoolboy, who had never seen him, turned to watch. So that dark guy is the famous Speedy Mason, they thought. Looks plenty tough, don't he? But old.

"Yessir," remarked Chisel, "he's a great one, that man. He's smart; he paces himself all the time, takes care of his health, and makes every pitch count. He's doing something with that ball, not just throwing it like some of these-here wild youngsters, burning it in every time. They got it to waste. Tell ya another, Casey, that Kid from Tomkinsville, number 34 over there, that man Tucker. A wonderful feller to have around; he can lift a club better'n anyone we got, know that? And thoughtful, too. I tell 'em and I tell 'em to bring in the batting helmets and the jackets and stuff on the bench after a game. I warn 'em it'll be pinched if they don't. Who comes in with his arms full every night? Why, Tucker, always Tucker with a load after every game."

Slowly the gang around Speedy dissolved; the men suited up and tromped out onto the field. Ballplayers realize that often when you ought to win, you lose. You feel free and easy, you're rested and eager and loose, but something goes wrong and you drop a game. You just don't have it. Why, nobody can tell.

That evening was one of them, an evening when the Dodgers lost a game they should have taken. So they left St. Louis with a 2-2 split, and although they grabbed a couple in Chicago they dropped the last game, when Schoolboy Johnson, after pitching magnificently, got into a dispute with the umpire over a close call and finally ended by dishing up a gopher ball with two down and a man aboard in the ninth. So there was another game gone that was practically in the bag.

The young pitcher thundered into the bedroom an hour after dinner, banging the door. Speedy Mason, who had been rooming with Johnson at the request of Spike Russell (though the Schoolboy didn't know this), glanced up from the easy chair where he had been reading the sports pages.

"Shoot!" said the big boy. "You go like a fire engine for twenty-six outs, those baboons get you a single run, then that-there stiff, that Crawford who bats .232 comes up, shuts his eyes, and golfs one."

The older man tossed the paper away. How many kids I've heard talk like that, he thought. Lose their temper and blame someone else for it. However, he said nothing. What he wanted to say was: Look, son, you pitched yourself a first-class game, but there in the ninth you got mixed up in that rhubarb with old Stubblebeard, and you lost your concentration. One strike was all you needed; you didn't pay attention, and boom! The guy leveled off on you.

Instead, he kept quiet. No use preaching.

The boy threw himself on one of the two beds. "Why, he just shut his eyes and swang. The lucky stiff, gets himself a Chinese homer, the big bum. Three hundred feet, that's what it measures to that fence in right, three hundred measly feet. Call this a ball park!"

I've seen worse, thought Speedy, remembering Macon and Savannah and a few others. Besides, it isn't three hundred feet; it's exactly three hundred and fifty-three to that fence there in right, as you ought to know. Maybe it was a good thing; maybe you learned a lesson out there today.

Then, in a sympathetic tone, he mumbled, "Yeah, hard luck all right. But a feller has to bear down on every pitch. Old Señor Menendez taught me that in the Mexican League."

"The Mexican League, hey?" The boy rose from the bed, leaned over, yanked open a bureau drawer, and pulled out some clean laundry. He laid three shirts out on the bed, and chose one carefully. Then he removed his coat and ripped off the shirt he wore. "So you played in the Mexican League! Where is that—in Mexico?"

"Yeah, it so happens. I was there two seasons. And when I was nineteen, I'd pitched two no-hitters in American Legion ball, but I got a big deal and lots of cash. I knew all there was to know, and I was so young my dad had to sign the contract for me."

"Thass so?" said the boy, his tone indicating complete lack of interest. His attention was riveted upon his figure in the mirror as he stood brushing his thick, blond hair, a military brush in each hand. He went at it diligently, stroking the yellow mane back from his forehead. He turned his head first to one side, then to the other, regarding himself up and down with care.

From the armchair Speedy Mason watched this performance. Was I like that once upon a time? he mused. Doesn't seem possible now, but I imagine I was.

Finally, giving his coat a last, vigorous tug about the shoulders, the boy appeared satisfied. "Guess I'll go down and get me a Black Cow."

"A what? Thought you never drank."

"Don't. A Black Cow is, well. . . . It's a root beer . . . and ice cream . . . and things." He flicked a piece of lint from his shoulder and gave one last tender look at the mirror.

Speedy rose and stretched, yawning. "Maybe I'll go

'long too. Sounds kinda interesting, that-there Black Cow."

"Oh?" The blond giant stopped short on his way to the hall door. "Oh, sure, only perhaps you wouldn't like it."

"Mebbe not, but I'll take a chance if you will."

"H'm. I see." He stood hesitating. "Well, to tell you the fact, Speedy, I've got a date, sort of."

"A date?"

"Yeah, kinda."

"O.K. Don't let Spike Russell see you."

"He won't. She has a car. We're going out to the Blue Bottle on Route 17."

"Just so you get home at a reasonable time. That night in St. Loo you rolled up at two A.M. You know, Spike Russell doesn't go much for that stuff."

"I see. I getcha." He removed his jacket and flung it with petulance across a chair. "O.K., Daddy-O, if that's how you feel about it. Let's all be good boys and go to bed at nine P.M. Kenny was different; when I roomed with Ken he made no never-minds what time I came in, so long as I didn't turn on the light and wake him up."

"Yeah. I'm not Kenny Preston."

"Yeah, I know. Kenny was a good roomie."

"Look, feller, when I came back up here, Jerry Sands bunked me in with you. I didn't ask this as a favor or draw you as a prize on a quiz program."

"Uh-huh, only you go squealing to the manager if a guy stays out after ten o'clock. I'm restless; I can't sleep."

"I haven't squealed, as you call it, yet. But I might, if you keep rolling in in the early hours the way you've been doing on this western trip."

" 'Course, Speedy, if you wanna play it that way, if you're gonna be a stinker, it's O.K. The boys all said you was a tough customer; they sure was right, too."

He stood there revealing his flat stomach. Speedy Mason immediately felt his slacks tight about his middle. I must quit eating potatoes, he thought. What wouldn't I give to be nineteen, with a belly like that and the things I know about pitching that he doesn't.

"I told you I haven't said a word. That don't mean I won't. I got no choice. Look at it this way: the pennant is up for grabs. Seven grand, that's the difference between first and second place. I need it if you don't. One thing more, my friend, when you go out on the town, you don't only hurt yourself, you hurt everyone on the club."

The boy immediately lost his self-control. "Aw, don't gimme that Sunday-school stuff. I wasn't born yesterday. I know my way round town." Suddenly he turned, his pajamas in his hand. Hate darkened his countenance. "Look, old-timer, don't hold on forever. You're keeping some good young pitcher down on the farm—ever think of that? And speaking as you were of the club, why'n you do us all a favor? Retire from baseball before baseball retires you."

The venom in his voice leaped at Speedy. He tried hard to keep his tone casual and conversational, taking time to light a cigarette before answering. They're always the same, these youngsters; maybe I was like that once, too. Who knows?

"Well, Schoolboy, pr'aps that's good advice; then again, pr'aps not. You haven't seen me pitch yet. Give a guy a break, wait till you see me throw. I'm chucking the opener in Cinci."

"Against Mayberry. No! That right? Why, there's one we hafta win, positively. He won't pitch you; he'll throw in Josh Crayton."

"Wrong again. He told me an hour ago, and I'm leaving by plane early tomorrow ahead of the team, so's I can rest up and be ready. I always go good in Cincinnati."

"He sure don't care how he loses the pennant, does he? Look, there's one more guy been round too long for his own good—that-there Spike Russell. Well, if he throws you in against those sluggers on the Redlegs, I'll give you five innings."

It hurt, though Speedy endeavored to conceal it. The caustic brutality of the boy cut deep. "So you think," he replied curtly.

"Tell you what, old-timer. I got twenty bucks says you won't last out the game, and most likely I'll be in there bailing you out, too."

"Say, you enjoy losing your cash, big boy. Suppose you might just as well fork it over instead of spending it on some babe. How about twenty on both counts? Maybe this'll prove to you that a guy isn't necessarily washed up when he's over nineteen."

"Why, fine! Twenty bucks on each count, that the Reds get you outa there, and that I'm relieving you. Pleased to take your dough, Speedy."

Later on, the lights out, they lay in their beds. It was the youngster who dropped off first. The old pitcher, his arms behind his head, watched the darkness break and the summer dawn come slowly in through the open window. Those words stayed with him.

"Why'n you retire from baseball before baseball retires you?"

Is this crazy kid repeating what's being said, what he's heard around the club, I wonder?

CHAPTER 8

Pitching in the Rain

It was raining hard the morning the rest of the team reached Cincinnati. By early afternoon the storm grew violent, so the game was postponed, and the battered Dodgers got a day's rest. They needed it. Sunny Jim was catching with a badly split thumb. Highpockets had a swollen right forearm where he had twice been struck by fast balls. Jackson Jones nursed a strained tendon in his heel and hobbled on the base paths. Red Allen, after playing in seventy-three straight games, was in a batting slump, and the whole pitching staff was sore and weary.

Most of all, this club which had boarded the Southwestern so confidently that night in New York only one game behind, was now three down with time running out. As they took the field the next day, every man knew what hung on those two games. Every man on the Dodgers was trying not to think of it, to shove it from his mind.

Why, this could be the day we lost the pennant!

It was the biggest gate of the year despite the threatening weather, a mob that jammed the streets leading to Crosley Field, that stood patiently in long lines at the ticket windows, a throng packing the seats and standing in rows four deep behind the tiers back of home plate. Those unable to see the diamond listened to pocket radios, reporting from time to time on the Milwaukee-Pittsburgh contest under way at that moment.

The Dodgers gave Speedy Mason an early lead when Highpockets homered into the right-field bleachers with two aboard in the first. Then, in the Cincinnati half of the second, the overcast skies began weeping. A drizzle started. There was a stir in the open stands in right field; newspapers shrouded heads and shoulders. Behind the plate, folks in the boxes down front began coming under the covered stands, clogging the aisles. The wind rose, the flagpole in center bent in the rain, damp newspapers fluttered onto the soggy grass of the outfield, the sky darkened. Then the deluge came, and the players scuttled for the dugouts like wet rats.

For an hour rain fell and the game was delayed. Inside the clubhouse the players changed their damp uniforms, played bridge, or listened to the Milwaukee game, while Doc Kastner, the trainer, massaged Speedy's arm with a horrible-smelling liniment from a bottle marked "Athletic Magic."

Finally the rain let up and a truck rumbled onto the field, dumping red dirt into the pools of water on the infield. Although the outfield was a morass, the lights were turned on and the game resumed. The scoreboard showed Milwaukee ahead by a run in the eighth.

Speedy's arm felt stiff, and they began hitting him—not hard, but well enough to get two men on base. Then a Cincinnati batter smacked a stinging bounder between the mound and short. Everyone on the field moved fast.

Speedy hustled for it. Ed Peters charged in; but Roy Tucker, cutting over rapidly from third, got there first. He reached up and ticked the ball, which roared off his glove over Peters' outstretched arm into the outfield. The ball rolled into a marsh in left center, halfway toward Highpockets, and died. Two runs came over, and the score was tied before they could retire the side.

Suddenly there was a burst of noise; a roar from the crowd swept the field. Everyone turned to the big scoreboard, where the result of the other game was flashed. Milwaukee had lost to Pittsburgh in the ninth, so this game the Dodgers had to win.

Milwaukee had dropped a vital contest. This was the time to recover lost ground, and the boys could almost smell the pennant. Out in the bull pen two reliefers were throwing hard now. It was only that veteran team's fine defense, their instinctive sense of the right play to make and the right throw in every play, that kept them in the running.

In the third, the first two batters singled; but Speedy got Carrington, the Redlegs' Negro slugger. After the next man popped up, Highpockets slogged through the water deep in left to snag a liner headed for the fences. In the fourth, a single and an intentional pass with one down had Speedy in trouble; again he made the next two batters fly out. In the sixth, with two out, Cincinnati filled the bases. But the old pitcher's control was sharp, and he made a dangerous hitter lift a foul that Roy Tucker gathered in close to the third-base boxes. The Dodgers got him three more runs in the seventh, and Brooklyn had a comfortable lead, 6-3.

Schoolboy Johnson, after his last exhibition, had been relegated temporarily to the bull pen. He sat watching every pitch, seeing Spike Russell stalk nervously up and down, weighing everything Speedy threw. Occasionally the big boy would suddenly stand and start burning them in to Fat Stuff; then as Speedy worked out of the jam, he would sit down and relax again. But all the time his eyes, his thoughts were on that man in the box, for he felt loose and longed to get into action. Surely, he said to himself, the old guy won't last another inning.

After a while, the rain began again, another slow drizzle. The air felt colder; folks huddled together in the bleachers.

"It's raining hard in downtown Cincinnati now," said the announcer, as the crowd groaned. Once more the boxes in front emptied, and out in the bleachers folks hunched under umbrellas and covered their soaked clothes with damp newspapers. Then the heavens opened, and the players, water streaming off their caps and down the back of their necks, broke for shelter.

They stood around the lockers in their underclothes, wiping themselves off with towels, hanging their wet things up to dry on hangers, Chisel running around with armfuls of soaking uniforms. It was frustrating, and the tension and the importance of that contest made the wait even more so. Nobody cared to play cards now. They slumped on the benches in disgust. If it hadn't been the team's last day in town on their final western trip, the game would obviously have been called off.

Spike beckoned Fat Stuff, the pitching coach, into his small room. "How's about it out there?"

"Isn't only one man for you now, Skip."

"You mean Josh Crayton?"

"Nope, I mean Johnson."

"Schoolie? Can't do it. Saving him for the opener against the Giants at the Polo Grounds."

"Yeah, I remember. But look, Spike, you better make darn sure of this one, or what happens against the Giants next week end won't matter. If you need someone, Schoolboy's the man. That hop on his fast one is vicious. I've been catching him; I can't hardly see it; won't none of those batters touch it, either."

Finally the rain let up, and they came out again through the murk onto the water-logged field. The haze from the lights above steamed with a thickish mist falling from the skies; it distorted everything. Speedy walked slowly to the mound. Despite the efforts of the trainer, he felt stiff. It showed, for he immediately gave up a base on balls. The next batter beat out a soppy roller. Instantly Spike trotted to the mound. "You're not chucking the way you were, Speedy."

"They're not hitting me badly; they haven't hit me all day. I'd like to stay in, Spike."

The manager patted him on the back and returned to the bench. His confidence seemed justified when Speedy got the Reds' pitcher on an infield fly. That left the big one, the important one, the one to make or break them, the one that could take them over the hump.

He threw in the curve and got a strike. He threw the slider and missed by inches only. All over the misty diamond the gang called to him, affection in their voices.

"Now then, Speedy."

"We'll get him, Speedy."

"Let him hit it; we'll get him for ya."

The stands were screaming for a hit, and the batter dug in and leaned over the plate. The pitch was high and close, and he tumbled into the mud. Watching from third, Roy Tucker knew exactly what that pitch meant. He knows they think he's tired, so he's saying: Look, you guys; I'm still in there throwing. Come and get me.

The pitcher blew on his hands, wiped them on his trousers, waved his arms to loosen his shirt, toed the rubber, and leaned over to watch the signals carefully. This was not the moment for any mix-up. Then he tossed in his let-up pitch, which had been fooling Cincinnati batters all afternoon.

The man at the plate met it and drilled the ball hard into the hole between right and center. Once again it died in a deep pond by the bleachers, and again two runs came across the plate.

Spike was on the dugout step, waving to the bull pen, before the runner reached second. There was only one out, the Dodgers were now but one run to the good, and this was a game they had to win. The big chap in the distant bull pen burned in several pitches casually, then turned, and, his jacket under his arm, walked toward the mound. His shoes squeaked and squelched as he came across the outfield turf.

Speedy Mason stood motionless, saw Sunny Jim come toward him, felt the catcher's hand rest affectionately on his damp shoulder. He handed over the ball. Then he walked slowly toward the dugout and the clubhouse and the warmth of the showers.

The crowd was yelling as the big Californian took the mound. This is for me, he thought, these conditions were made to order. He tossed in a few to his catcher, thinking, Here's where I really show the old man up. And take his money, too.

The rain-soaked crowd in the stands called to Carrington, the Redleg slugger, for a hit that would tie the game. On the mound Schoolboy Johnson faced him confidently. The setup was made to order for him; he had it and he knew it. His first pitch blazed in low, by the knees, so fast the crowd behind the plate responded with a long "Oh. . . ."

Then he burned the next one across for the strike. Hope old Mason is watching. He'll see what a real pitcher is, not an old has-been who's been around too long for his own good.

The batter swung at the pitch, got a piece of it, and hit it into the air, where it was lost in the haze above. Sunny Jim turned, half slipped, recovered his footing, went back in the mud, feeling the mist on his bare face. He peered up into the murk, saw the descending ball, and caught it.

With two men gone, the Schoolboy felt better. Now he really was on top. He simply poured in the next three pitches, so fast the batter didn't see them until they were past. Strike one. Strike two. Strike three. The side was out.

The team poured into the shelter of the bench, wet, panting, happy. "Nice chucking, Schoolie."

"Great throwing, feller, great throwing out there."

"You showed 'em something, Schoolboy! Stick it down their throats now."

That last inning he really did show them. Two Redleg hitters never even took their bats from their shoulders. Then he struck out the last man on a called strike, to make five in the two innings.

Speedy heard it from the radio beside the rubbing table,

where Doc was working over him. Jerry Sands, the club secretary, passed by the door, and he called out.

"Hey, Jerry, do me a favor. Let me have forty bucks, will you please?"

"Forty bucks? You can't spend any tonight, Speedy. We got that plane chartered to take the club home."

"I know, I know. I'm not going out on the town; I just need it. Let's say I dropped it in a card game, hey?"

The other man looked at him with a queer glance. What's biting him, he wondered. Usually Speedy Mason is as tight as a clam's tail. He won't even spend money for taxis; he's a family man, holds on to his dough. I know he doesn't play cards, either. What's up? He never bets on the horses. Well, it's none of my business.

So he replied, "Why sure, Speedy, if you say so. It's kind of irregular. With some of the boys I wouldn't do this, but I guess if you need it, that's sufficient. Here ya are, four tens. Right?"

"Thanks, Jerry. I won't forget it."

CHAPTER 9

Nursemaid to a Young Pitcher

"Wouldn't attempt to argue with you about it, Speedy; you know your family and your responsibilities better'n I do. You may be able to take a chance on losing ten thousand bucks. I feel you're making a mistake."

Roy Tucker sat with Speedy Mason in his room in the hotel after dinner.

"Maybe. As you say, it's a lot of cash. But there are times when a man must think about himself. Point is, I can't take this any more; what between that Schoolboy and not getting a chance to pitch regularly, it's too much." He rose, stretched, lit a cigarette, and slipped on his coat.

Just then the key turned in the lock, and the big blond boy, wearing a natty new sports jacket, burst into the room. "S'cuse me, old-timers, won't be a minute. Just popped in to clean up and change my clothes."

Roy Tucker's eyebrows went up. He glanced over at Speedy, whose lips were shut tight around his cigarette, a strange look on his face. "Enjoy yourself, son; the place is all yours. We were just going out, anyway."

He and Speedy went down in the elevator together and got off at the twelfth floor. Roy paused and then held out his hand. "Wish you wouldn't, Speedy. I sure wish you wouldn't. You know you and Red are really the only old-timers left now, the only ones I can talk to, and Red, he don't talk, except to say, 'Pass the salt.' But however it works out and whatever happens, good luck all the way."

They shook hands. "Thanks, Roy, I sure hate to leave, only it has to be." Speedy turned and walked slowly down the hall while Roy rang for the elevator. At a door marked 1214-15, he finally stopped and knocked.

"Come in." The manager was in an armchair, his feet on a davenport, newspapers about the floor. Fat Stuff was standing at his side.

"Oh! Excuse me, I thought you were alone, Spike."

"Come on, Speedy, come in. I'm just leaving, just going. Right, Skipper, that's for sure, eh?"

"Yes, Fat Stuff, and you can quote me."

"Good. So long, Speedy." He left, shutting the door behind him.

Spike Russell looked up, noticed the serious expression on his visitor's face. "Take a load offa your dogs, old-timer."

"Thanks, I will. Fact, that's what I came in to see you about, Spike."

"About what, Speedy?"

"About taking a load off my feet, about sitting down. Seems that's about all I been doing since I came back up here."

"Why, Speedy, that isn't true. You pitched that game in the rain in Cincinnati; you won that one for us and it was a mighty important one. . . ."

"I did *not*." His voice was sharp, with a ring in it. "Let's not kid around. Schoolie won it. A first-class job he turned in, too."

"I know, I know, Speedy, this pitching staff is in and out. Over at Milwaukee they fell to pieces, now they're hot as a pistol. You're mighty important to this club."

"As nursemaid to a boy wonder."

"Put it that way if you like." He smiled. "You been through the mill; I hoped you could show him a few things."

"Spike, lemme give it to you straight. Take it from me, nobody could get anything into that head of his with a pickax. He *knows*. But forget it. It's me I came in about. This bull-pen stuff is no good. I want to go back."

The manager sat up straight and stared. "To Augusta? You crazy?"

Speedy shook his head. "Nope, I mean it."

Spike Russell uncorked his long legs, walked across the room, picked up a book, and thumbed it through. "Look, here's the latest *Baseball Guide*. Page 178 . . . World Series . . . 'Winner's share, $9746.35.' Nine-ten thousand bucks you're chucking away. You must be a millionaire."

"You know darn well that isn't true. I need the money, who doesn't? But this is something else, it's my life. I have to pitch, Spike, like some of the boys have to eat all the time and some have to play the races. 'Cept for that game in Cincinnati, I've been out in the bull pen. Spike, *I have to pitch.*" The intensity in his tone was reflected in the serious look on his dark face.

"We can hold you until the end of the season, Speedy. We can use you as we think best, bull pen or no bull pen."

"Sure, only that isn't your way of doing business. Look, Skip, lemme get back where I can play. I'd be a help to those boys; they're green, but they're learning. If I go back we'll make the play-offs."

"The play-offs! Five-six hundred bucks, and up here you have a chance at 10,000. Might be your last chance, too, feller."

"Don't rub it in, Spike."

"Sorry, old-timer, forget that one. I'm sorry." Of all the tough things they hand you, here's one of the hardest. Baseball is a business; sentiment is out—if you want to survive. You must be impersonal, bring 'em up and send 'em down. A player has to prove himself out there on the field and do it alone. But this veteran is different. No matter what he may claim, I think he keeps that slap-happy young pitcher from going out too much at night. Anyhow, the kid's improvement dates from the moment they started to room together, even if Speedy denies it. Right now I don't need him too badly, I have four pitchers in good shape, they've all come around at the same time; we aren't badly off like the Phils and the Cards. But suppose one goes sour! What then? Or am I making too much of this? Is he really necessary to us?

Spike looked ahead, speculating, trying to see those last, vital moments of the campaign. "Speedy, let's us try to get together on this thing. I need you badly in the bull pen; you're an old-timer, you're steady, you don't rattle. I know how sick you are of that kid, I understand it, I don't blame you. . . ."

"I want to play baseball, Skip. I want to pitch in rotation. I told Roy Tucker when he came up to give it to you straight. I told him to say I needed work, lots of work, regular work, not a bull-pen job."

"Sure, he did; he did. I understand how you feel."

And there's another big-leaguer, that Tucker. They both get out before anyone else, they take batting practice, they throw batting practice, they do their laps around the park, they fill in at second or short when the substitute infield works out. Pros—that's what they are.

"Another thing, Spike. I've seen 'em come and go, but this boy just doesn't think major-league. Maybe will some day, he sure don't now, and I can't do anything with him. But so far's I'm concerned, I'd room with whoever you say if it would help the club any. It's not that. . . ."

The phone rang and Spike rose angrily. With a touch of annoyance in his tone, he answered. "Operator, thought I said not to ring me this evening." There was a frown on his forehead. "What? What? What hospital? Who? Yes, sure, of course, put him right on." He stood a long minute holding the telephone.

Speedy distinguished a man's voice, heard Spike say "Yes . . . uh-huh . . . that's correct. That's me. Why yes, doctor, he is. He's one of our boys. I say he's one of our pitchers. What happened? He did? When? Is it bad? It is? Oh, I see, I getcha." He listened a long time as the voice at the other end of the line continued. "All right, I'll be up directly. I'll be right along. And thanks for calling me."

Putting down the telephone, he turned. "With this bunch if it isn't one thing, it's another. Cassidy. He's in Roosevelt Hospital."

"Cassidy?" Speedy Mason rose as Spike grabbed for his jacket and stuffed his wallet into his pocket. "What happened, Spike? Is he badly hurt?"

"Don't know for certain. A taxi accident. He's busted two ribs and right now he's unconscious."

CHAPTER 10

Accident to a Fender

Schoolboy Johnson stalked across the street from the club-house entrance to the parking lot, talking furiously to himself.

"Call that easy fly a hit! Why, any ordinary bush-league fielder would have gobbled it. That's what comes of having sports writers for official scorers. Those guys and their silly questions! What'd you give him to hit, what did he crack that homer offa, yakety-yak-yak. They get buddy, those sports writers, they all have their pals; then when their turn comes to be official scorer, they protect them. This is what a guy is up against. As for those old-timers, all of a sudden they ain't got it any more. Lack of speed kills 'em. Yep, kills the pitcher, too. Except for that stupid Karl Case, I'd have a no-hitter now."

Angry and disappointed, he strode over to his car. "Why'n the official scorer have the guts to call 'em as they are; an error's an error no matter who makes it and who

gets hurt. Case shoulda had his mitts on that ball. Ten
years ago, nothing to it. Give Case an error, and my no-
hitter would be in the books now, my first month in the
majors."

He eased himself slowly into the long, low, black car.
As a rule, following an afternoon game, he was pestered
by kids; but his parley with the sports writers, his shower,
his long rubdown had consumed considerable time. It was
late in the afternoon and only a handful of cars were left
in the parking lot. Most of them, he knew, belonged to
the players still in the clubhouse. No youngsters were
visible. Schoolboy Johnson felt neglected, which added
to his annoyance.

Shoot, if it hadn't been for that old man in right, I'd had
a no-hitter—my first month in the big time, too.

He swung the car quickly out of the parking lot, gunned
the motor, and turned sharply up the empty street. Immediately a nasty grinding noise, the unpleasant sound of
metal scraping on metal, attacked his ears.

He slowed down, glanced over his shoulder. A tall
girl jumped from a car standing beside the curb at the
entrance to the parking lot from which he had just turned
out.

Moving to the curb ahead, he yanked savagely at the
hand brake and got out. I'll tell her off. Look, lady, signs
all over the place; you got no right parking there. You
can read.

She swung about, a sun-burned girl with an attractive,

intelligent face, her black hair off her forehead, watching him as he came toward her, with a curious look. The closer he got the less he felt like telling her off. After all. . . .

Because by her look and the way she sized him up from his well-combed blond hair to the fitted slacks and the tan shoes with white uppers, he knew immediately she guessed who he was.

Well, naturally. . . .

"Sorry, lady, must have been asleep that time. Car hurt bad?"

"You dented the fender. It's only a scratch, but I imagine it will have to come off to be repaired."

Together they bent over the injured fender. A faint scent came from the girl's hair; he liked it. Then he inspected the fender. It had been slightly bent but not broken. A minor job, yet he knew she was right. They'd probably have to take the whole fender off. That means time. In a garage, time is money.

He walked to his car and got out his papers. His own car appeared to be undamaged; even his bumper showed no signs of contact. He glanced up and down the little side street, usually swarming with cops before, during, and after a game. Not an officer was visible—or anyone else. Even the parking-lot attendant had packed up for the day.

A thought struck him. This would be one fine angle for some cheap sports writer after a story. Schoolboy

Johnson saw the headline, maybe even a front-page story.

"Dodger Player Smashes Girl's Car."

They'd have the automobile in pieces and the girl in a hospital, maimed for life.

"See here, lady," he said, returning with his papers in his hand. "You do what you like, and my insurance company will take care of the damage, but I'd be glad to save time and trouble and handle the whole thing myself. What say we get an estimate from a garage this evening, and I'll settle with you right away?"

He turned it on full force, giving her the small-boy-in-trouble technique which he had always found worked well. She had, he observed with interest, a fashion-model figure.

She returned his glance without, he thought, much enthusiasm. Could it be she didn't know who he was?

"Fair enough, only you'll have to wait for my father. You must fix things up with him; he owns the car, not me. He'll be along shortly."

He grinned. "O.K., I'll wait. Hope he's as nice as you are."

"How could he help it?" She turned her back and climbed in behind the wheel. His face fell and, noticing this, she said in a kinder tone, "I'll admit I shouldn't strictly be parked here; there were no-parking signs around. But it was late and I expected Dad any minute."

He leaned on the side of the door. A good-looker. Her figure was still more impressive close to. Don't care if the old man never comes. So he turned it on full strength. "You're sure kind. Some folks go into a tizzy even when rain falls on their car. See the game?"

She lit a cigarette. "Nope. I'm a working girl."

Aha! Now he was sure she didn't know him. So much the better.

"That right? What line?"

"Oh. . . . I'm a window designer."

"How's that? You design windows?"

"No, I just arrange them, change the displays every week, and so on. The Pan-Am window on Fifth Avenue, and the British Tourist Office on Madison are two of my accounts. Doesn't leave time for ball games. Besides, I saw a game, once."

She shot him a quick glance, observing that some of his cockiness (or was it merely assurance?) had vanished. He was shocked. Also he was quite certain she didn't know him from the president of the National League.

"Lady, you got it wrong. Baseball's different, something new every day, new plays, new strategy, new situations, never the same thing twice. Now, f'rinstance, take the game today. You didn't happen to catch it on the air? Nope? Well, seems the pitcher has a no-hitter going into the ninth." He paused and glanced down to see her gazing at him. "Know what that means?"

She smiled. "Father explained it to me once."

"Oh, I see. Well, now, this poor guy has a no-hitter going, with two down in the ninth—think of it! One out from a no-hitter. All spoiled by an old-time outfielder who hasn't got it any more—'course he don't realize this. Probably that no-hitter would be worth coupla thousand more at contract time next year to the pitcher. So . . . all shot because of this veteran out there in right field."

Now she knew who he was talking about and *she* was shocked. This girl did not care to think of Karl Case as being through at thirty-five. He was a ballplayer known for always doing his job and doing it well, making it seem easy, even—with no color or drama such as Highpockets or Jackson Jones managed to convey, but a real pro just the same.

All the time the Schoolboy was talking earnestly. "Y'see, lady, what these old-timers, these vets, don't realize is, they're keeping some smart kid down on a farm club that ought to be up here getting experience."

"Oh, I see, I understand. Hadn't thought about that point. Guess I've always liked the old-timers best."

He leaned closer and flashed his smile, a smile that could undo most women. "Why, sure you do, everyone does, all the fans do; they go for the old-timers. Now I'll tell ya why. They've watched these fellers, seen 'em play year after year; they get kinda fond of 'em in a way, you might almost say like old friends. I know how it is. Take you, if you have a favorite on the Dodgers. . . ."

He hesitated a moment, hoping, even after her last remark that she would say, "Me, oh, I go for this young speed-baller, this artist. . . ."

"Guess you're correct. I go for Roy Tucker."

He swallowed his disappointment. Wait till she sees me out there, he thought. "There ya are! Same as all the fans. Roy Tucker, a nice guy, none better, everyone on the club likes him. But look, lady, he shouldn't be out there on third, nor would be if Martin hadn't busted his leg last month. No ma'am, no indeedy. Look at it another way. Think of that poor pitcher chucking his heart out this afternoon, throwing a no-hitter almost, then with two strikes on that man the last of the ninth, losing it all. A no-hitter. . . ."

Reverence came into his voice as he repeated the phrase. "A no-hitter. The most beautiful thing—"

"I always imagined a homer with the bases full was the best of all," she interjected, no reverence at all in her tone.

"Nothing to it!" he snapped back. "Happens all the time. But a no hitter is a bee-yootiful, bee-yootiful thing."

She looked at him closely, saw his face, realized what it meant to him. Though he was a rookie ballplayer, somewhere deep inside him was the soul of a poet.

"A man said it a long while ago. 'A thing of beauty is a joy forever.' "

Schoolboy Johnson was watching Karl Case's outstretched glove miss that ball by a yard. It was a fly he would have had in his pocket a few years ago. Then the Schoolboy returned quickly to the present. "Yeah . . . I guess *so*. Only a no-hitter stays in the record books for good and all."

" 'A thing of beauty is a joy forever . . . it will never pass into nothingness.' That's how a poet said it once."

Instantly he was alert. "Go on! No kidding! You say a poet wrote that? Talking of sport, was he?"

"Well," she smiled up at him, a charming, warm smile, an altogether delightful smile, one of the nicest smiles this collector of smiles from young ladies had ever seen. "Not exactly. But then again, he might have been, who knows; sport is beauty too."

He liked that smile, and the way she laughed, and the strange things she said, and most of all the pleasant intimacy that had developed between them so suddenly. For a second these two human beings came together emotionally.

Then the illusion of intimacy dissolved, and they were far apart. For coming straight toward them, across the street, he noticed Roy Tucker.

Shoot, hope the old gent doesn't see me. He might find out about the accident and tell the gang. Then tomorrow every sports writer in town will have me running over this girl at sixty-five miles an hour. So the Schoolboy hastily presented his back to his teammate and crouched down toward the open window, waiting for him to move past to his own car.

Unfortunately, instead of going past, the third baseman

only came closer. Schoolie could even make out his foot-
steps getting louder, louder, louder.

Then a hand fell on his shoulder. "Hi there, Schoolboy!"

"Daddy, this gentleman smacked your car," remarked
the girl casually.

Schoolboy Johnson cringed. The veteran removed his
hand hastily, stepped back, and surveyed the dent in the
rear fender. "I'll say he did!"

About half an hour later, the garage visited, the arrange-
ments concluded, and twenty-two and a half dollars of
Speedy's cash having changed hands, the young pitcher
bent over to say good-by to the girl. After all, he thought,
she has possibilities.

"So long for now, then," he said. "You'll be seeing me
later."

She looked up at him and smiled. Yet her words had a
sting. "I can hardly wait," she said.

Soon Roy Tucker and his daughter were driving along
the parkway. "Oh, but Dad, if you could have seen his
face when he realized you were my father! It was so
funny. Well, I can see what you mean about him, Dad.
But yet and all...." She edged closer to him in the driver's
seat, taking his arm. "Y'know, you really can't hate the
boy."

"Why not? Speedy Mason, who rooms with him, manages to."

"Oh, I'm sure he could be a pest if you had him as a roomie. But he's kinda cute just the same."

Roy Tucker glanced quickly at his daughter. Her eyes had a distant look, and he knew she was watching a tall boy with thick blond hair, in a natty sports jacket, with an assured, self-satisfied manner, who leaned down into her car window.

"Cute! That fresh young busher!"

"Oh, Daddy, you forget. You were a busher yourself once."

"Why certainly, we all were. Only not like this young punk, though."

Whatever possesses women, he wondered, as he drove along. Over a fair number of years, he had observed that they often went for the wrong ones.

Cute! Cute! Isn't that something? Cute! One hundred and ninety pounds in shorts and wooden shower clogs, six feet two inches in his socks, and this girl of mine, who knows baseball and ballplayers as well as anyone, calls him cute.

"Besides, what's cute about him? I don't get it."

CHAPTER 11

Throwing the Change-up

The end of August, and the Dodgers clinging to second place, a full game out of first. You could wake up the next morning leading the league, or you could lose and find yourself sitting in third, ready to slide lower still. Consequently each game had to be won, each contest was a must. Yet this was the one they especially wanted and every man on the club realized it.

Speedy Mason was pitching. He had started once before and won; a lot depended on how he shaped up this afternoon. The fans knew it also, and they cheered when Speedy began to warm up. In the front row of a box beside the Dodger dugout, a girl in a flowered dress and a big hat, a girl who understood baseball and ageing ballplayers better than most men did, was rooting for him too. A tall player in a windbreaker leaning back on the bench, his long legs stretched out carelessly, peered with attention at the field—although he was leading no cheers for Speedy Mason.

The team tossed the ball about mechanically, their talents diminished, because now they were playing from instinct, almost from memory, with fire and spirit high, but with weary muscles and aching bones. The youngsters among them, like Ed Peters, the shortstop, and Jackson Jones in center and Schoolboy Johnson, seemed almost out of place in this line-up of veteran stars.

Here was a team meeting its greatest test and making its finest run for the money, a team apparently over the hill, yet still in there scrapping for the lead. Everyone except Jackson Jones had been disappointing at the plate most of the season; the homers with which they used to win important games came seldom, their sluggers had calmed down, the big blows were exceptional. Now this was a club hitting mostly singles and doubles.

Yet they still had the skill and the brains, the alert pitching and the solid defense. They never juggled balls or made the throw to the wrong base; they knew what they were doing every minute, which was why they were close to the leaders in the vital moments of the campaign.

This afternoon they faced the Cards, a second-division team. The Cards, anxious, like everyone else, to humble the Dodgers in their feverish race for the pennant, had saved the best pitcher they possessed for this game. But class told. It was Roy Tucker who singled in the third and Red Allen, another veteran, who brought him across with a double high off the fence in right. Sunny Jim then laced a liner into center and the Dodgers were off to a two-run lead.

On the mound Speedy Mason, who was too old for Montreal and not good enough for Elmira, held them off inning after inning. At times he was rescued by his out-fielders, ranging back to make impossible one-handed grabs near the fences; at times he stood watching as his opponents were wiped out by that lightning-fast double play his infield made so well. Ahead 2-0, they came into the top of the ninth with a pinch hitter up for the Cardinal hurler.

Astride the mound, Speedy was tired but confident. He had shut the door hard and was enjoying himself. Deftly he slipped his curve over the corner and got the batter, swinging on a third strike. Sunny Jim waddled out to hand him the ball as the Card lead-off man, a powerful hitter, came up. Speedy stood there, sweat on his uniform, his face, his arms. He nodded to the catcher and threw in the change-up.

The batter caught a piece of the ball, sending a slow roller toward short. Roy darted over as it went past, saw Ed Peters come charging in from the grass at deep short, handling the ball gracefully, gunning his throw across the diamond. Seconds counted, because the batter was a speed boy and the throw was close, so close it could have been called either way.

But the hands of the umpire were down, and the man was safe.

They stood around pretending to argue with Stubble-beard, back of first. Red Allen kicked the bag and slapped the ball into his glove. Sunny Jim, who raced over to back them up, protested; Bobby Russell joined them, shaking his head. Of course what they were doing was giving their pitcher a breather. They wanted him to win as much as he did.

Spike Russell stood with one knee on the top step of the dugout, leaning against a post, his favorite position during a game.

In the box beside the dugout the girl tugged at the edges of her big hat. Suddenly, with the sound of bat meeting ball, she covered her eyes with her hands. She knew baseball; she didn't need to look.

"Oh-oh," she said. "Oh-oh!"

The liner zoomed over second base, rising in flight, rising, rising like a bullet into the upper deck in center field. Jackson Jones, hands on hips, back toward the plate, stood under the wall, staring up at it. The ball struck an iron stanchion, bounded high into the air, and fell into a mass of scrambling kids.

The score was tied now, 2-2. The bull-pen pitchers, in action all through the last few innings, were throwing furiously. Slap-slap, slap-slap, slap-slap, went the ball from catcher to pitcher. Slap-slap, slap-slap. Would Spike beckon to them?

Behind home plate the crowd rose, peering down at him. The girl in the box leaned over and looked across curiously. Every eye was focused on the Brooklyn dug-out, and on Spike Russell leaning against that post as though nothing had happened to change the game—and perhaps the future of Speedy Mason.

Was he yanking the old pitcher? Would he be taken out, perhaps finished forever with major-league ball? Or would he stay in and possibly be belted out, with the game gone? Make the wrong decision, guess wrong, and the game you expected to win is lost forever.

Motionless, the manager stood against the post; motion-less he remained, even when the next batter singled. The bull pen kept on working; the balls went back and forth, slap-slap, slap-slap. Then the man astride the rubber took the ball from Ed Peters and leaned over the rosin bag, panting.

Spike Russell turned to the bench and beckoned to Schoolboy Johnson, who didn't see him. The Schoolie was in dreamland. This annoyed Spike, who always in-sisted that his pitchers especially watch every move on the diamond and follow every play.

"Johnson!" he called sharply. "Johnson! On your feet!"

Expecting to be sent down to the bull pen, Schoolie jumped. Spike, on the top step, leaned over and said, "Get a load of this old guy out there now. I want you to watch him carefully, see how he controls himself. This is a tough spot—one more hit and he comes out; he knows it.

See how he handles himself. Why can't you do the same thing, huh? Watch him carefully!"

With a nod of the head he dismissed the Schoolboy, who went back to the bench, subdued and somewhat dismayed.

Speedy, on the mound, was angry. He was upset, but he kept himself well in hand and knew what he was doing every minute. A piece of the plate and a called strike. A wasted ball just missing the corner. Another curve, at which the batter swung and hit sharply to Bobby Russell. The lead man was out, but the throw to first was late; there were two down and still a runner on base.

Once again, with all his immense skill and all his cunning, Speedy went to work, keeping the ball low. The batter watched the curve slice the corner, swung savagely, and missed. He took a ball, then hit the next pitch exactly as Speedy intended, a nice bounding roller toward second base.

Speedy didn't wait. He walked off the mound and moved toward the dugout before the play was finished. As he slumped down on the bench he slapped his glove against his leg with annoyance.

"Shoot!" he mumbled, half to himself and half to Doc beside him, massaging his reddened right arm. "Shoot, I have 'em eating out of my hand, three hits in nine innings, then I gotta get careless and the score is tied!" He paused, looked up, peered out. "Hey there, Jackson, attaboy, Jackson!"

Jackson Jones was rounding first with a nicely placed hit. Now the St. Louis bull pen was throwing feverishly, as Red Allen strode to the plate. With first open, they passed him to get at Sunny Jim—a poor move. For the catcher caught hold of the first pitch and lofted it into Bedford Avenue. The game was over.

Clatter-clatter, clatter-clatter, their spikes sounded on the concrete runway as they swarmed into the lockers, hot, tired, happy, everyone laughing and chattering. Reporters immediately surrounded Speedy sitting on the bench before his locker drinking Seven-Up from a bottle. They asked the usual questions.

"I should have my head examined. I figgered that was the spot for a change-up. He outguessed me, that's all; the ball hung there and he murdered it. I threw the curve to the last two men; no problem. What's that? The difference coming up the second time? Well, the second time you aren't frightened; you know what you're trying to do, even if you don't always do it. You've had it; you're hard to scare."

Roy Tucker, peeling off his clammy uniform, was talking to Casey of the *Mail*. "That number 32 out there, that Speedy Mason, he's the guy who has it. Just wait, Casey, he'll win four or five more for us, and believe me, with Cassidy lost from that accident, we're mighty darn lucky to have him. He's in there fighting every minute, nothing gets him down, and he gives you everything he's got every time he pitches."

Sunny Jim sat on a straight wooden chair receiving a barrage of handshakes and backslaps. He yanked the soggy bandages from his injured thumb, swollen and angry. "What kinda ball did I hit? Fast ball, shoulder-high, right where I like it. Yes sir, that's the one to win, believe me. I tell ya, let an old horse loose, and he's mighty hard to put that harness onto again. It's tough to catch him."

The team had swarmed inside; but one player in a windbreaker, a tall boy with blond hair, stepped into the crowd and walked to a nearby box as people poured onto the field. He leaned over a girl in a big hat, sitting in the front row.

"How're you today, lady? Some game the old guy pitched for himself, hey?"

She looked up, and he couldn't decide whether her glance was entirely friendly. Nor could he tell how much she knew about the different players on the club and their relations to each other. Her father might have said things; on the other hand, some ballplayers never talk off the field, even to their wives. Especially to their wives.

"Oh, hello there. Yes, he's quite a pitcher still, isn't he?"

The Schoolboy had no burning desire to pursue this subject. He shifted quickly. "Car all right now? No hard feelings 'bout that accident, I hope."

"None whatever. The garage straightened the fender

in a couple of hours. They said it was lucky the door wasn't hit; doors cost money to repair."

"Good." He stood looking down, hesitating a moment. But she seemed more attractive than ever, and after all, you can't arrest a man for trying. "Then pr'aps your old man'll let you come out and have dinner with me."

She glanced up, pulling the sides of her hat. The crowd surged past, curiously eyeing the ballplayer and the girl.

With coolness she answered. "I don't know how he'd feel. Daddy always says to watch out for wild young pitchers. Would I be perfectly safe with you?"

He looked at her closely. She had a large mouth and wide, brown eyes which he liked. The eyes were fixed on him. He also liked girls who looked his way.

"Safe with me? Definitely not." There was a kind of challenging note in his voice; he was a small boy inviting you to kick his cap, which he had just placed over a brick.

"Good," she replied instantly. "Then I'll be glad to come. When you go in to change, tell my father not to wait."

CHAPTER 12

How to Throw One Away

Like the Cards and every other team in the league, the Giants had reserved their pitching ace for the Dodgers, when they appeared at the Polo Grounds. Why not? Pennant contenders expect this treatment; they get it whether they like it or not. Nonetheless, always finding another club's star hurler rested and pointed for you gets tiresome. Each series becomes a dogfight. It didn't make the going any easier these hot days and nights.

This evening, with first place so close they could reach out and touch it, the game was tight all the way. An early run for New York, one for the Brooks, then Highpocket's triple in the fifth, after which he scored, and a second tally for the Giants. In the seventh, the home team went ahead 3-2. With the Dodger half of the eighth, a chance came to blow the game apart.

Jackson Jones spanked a double into left field. He was immediately advanced to third as Karl Case managed to beat out a dribbler to short, but the Giants kept Jackson from scoring. Men were on first and third with nobody out when Roy Tucker, the old reliable, came to bat. Their fastest runner was ninety feet from the plate and their best clutch hitter was facing the pitcher.

So Spike Russell put the sign on. It went from the bench to Micky Forbes, the third-base coach. He edged toward Jackson on the base path and spoke two words in his ear. To Roy, stepping into the batter's box, he flashed the sign—dangerous with the opposing ball club watching carefully. Roy, striding in, slung away the loaded bat, and as he did so his attention was distracted by the Giant catcher.

"Gonna bunt on us, Roy? Go ahead, we're ready."

The Dodgers had three signs: one for the ordinary bunt; one for the safety squeeze, in which the man on base takes his lead but waits for the bunt to go; and last of all the suicide squeeze, the all-or-nothing play, which Spike had ordered. Roy, half his attention on the catcher, failed to watch the coach closely as he gesticulated back of third. So he took the sign to mean a safety bunt.

On the second pitch Jackson took a dancing lead and went into a sprint for home. Roy, surprised, stabbed at the ball; but it was wide, and since he was not in the right position, he missed it completely. If he had connected and dropped it down the base path, Jackson could have come home standing up. As it was, he found himself hung up twenty feet from the plate.

The crowd rose, roaring, as his spikes dug in and he reversed himself. The diamond went into action; everyone was running. The Giant second baseman moved toward the bag, the shortstop came racing down to cover third, while the third baseman, taking a snap throw from the catcher, advanced with menacing arm on Jackson, dancing along halfway to the plate—back and forth, back and forth, the catcher and the third baseman converging on him every second. Suddenly, when the ball was in the air, he dashed past the catcher for the plate.

Standing astride it, the pitcher waited coolly. Taking a quick throw from the third baseman, he leaned over and slapped the ball on the sliding runner. Then, whirling, he drew back and whipped a strike to second base.

Karl Case, who had made his turn, was five feet off the bag, caught cold.

The crowd cheered as the infielders raced across to cover up, now concentrating on Karl, who edged up and down the base path, head erect, eyes alert, waiting for a hurried toss, a fumble, a chance to reach safety. Silently, grimly, they went to work on him with a kind of mechanical efficiency, snapping the ball to each other as only big-leaguers do in a critical moment.

Slap . . . slap . . . slap . . . it went from the second baseman to the shortstop and back again to the second baseman.

Then the latter, taking the ball, feinted a throw and suddenly lit out at full speed after the runner. Karl turned and sprinted for third, but the other man had the jump on him, and overhauled him fifteen feet from the bag. He was tagged, the double play was completed, the rally snuffed out in a matter of seconds. The next batter flied out, and what had been a big inning in the making was over and done with.

Twenty minutes later they tromped silently up the steps of the clubhouse in center, those stairs pitted and scarred by thousands of spikes, and into the coolness of the locker room. Yanking at their wet uniforms, they tugged off their shirts and sat morosely staring across the room, too weary to strip and pile into the showers, numbed by unexpected defeat.

You win, you're loose and full of gags and jokes, all good humor and happiness. You drop a game, especially if it's one you must have, and nobody has a word to say. You just sit there thinking, Why'n the Skipper play it safe? A fly ball would have tied the score. Whatever happened to Tucker? How come he missed that sign? Why did Karl get caught flat-footed out there at second?

At last, one by one, they chucked off their shoes, pulled at their trouser belts, tossed their socks and stockings to Chiselbeak, and moved toward the showers. This, they all knew, had been a game they should have won, a game it really hurt to lose.

The man who felt it most was Roy Tucker.

Speedy Mason had done his running, thrown a while, and then sat on the bench, but he was hot and sticky, so he went in to the showers. As he came out, a huge towel around his waist, he saw his pal still sitting despondent on the bench before his locker. He went over, sat down, and put his arm around Roy's shoulders.

"Never mind, feller."

Roy's head was slumped between his knees, and Speedy realized that he was hurt and sore. "No matter, Roy, you messed up a sign, but that's not the first time nor the last, most likely. We all do. Just remember these things happen to everyone, any moment in a game."

"Spike should hit me with a great, smacking fine. It's inexcusable missing a signal like that, inexcusable. That man and his yakety-yak, he sure outsmarted me." He chuckled grimly, shook his head, leaned over, and with an effort unlaced his shoes, kicking them off.

"Forget it, Roy, just forget it. You been in this game a long while, you know tomorrow's another day."

But Roy Tucker was inconsolable. He shook his head again and again. "Yeah. Only right now we haven't many tomorrows to waste. Y'know, Speedy, if I hadn't of missed that sign, I'd have been squared round for the pitch like I should have been. Shucks, after that great game Jim Mitchell pitched, too, what a way to let him down. How'd they do, how many hits, four . . . five? And we got eight. Speedy, boy, we're not getting that insurance run the way we usta. Like me missing that bunt, and all those men stranded on base. Too many left aboard, too many."

"Well, sure, only it isn't just that. Roy, the guys aren't

having themselves the big year any more. Imagine High-pockets batting .268, and Red and Case way down, too. C'mon now, shake yourself out of those wet clothes and get into the showers. No good sitting round being sorry for yourself."

Roy stood up. Over in a corner, Schoolboy Johnson was carefully tying his necktie. It was a brilliantly striped tie, obviously new, obviously expensive. He stood in his shirt sleeves before the mirror, straight, tall, thin-waisted. His tie tied, he took a comb from a small leather case in his pocket and combed his thick, blond mane thoroughly and carefully.

The two older men watched with a kind of fascinated interest. "Look at him, twenty years old and time stretching ahead. Looka that, Roy, what wouldn't you give to be twenty again?"

Roy Tucker directed his gaze across the room, watched the tall boy tenderly stroking his thick hair.

"Twenty!" he said. "What wouldn't I give to be thirty-five again!"

CHAPTER 13

A Game Is Nine Innings

Roy Tucker was astonished to see his daughter in the Dodger box the next afternoon at the Polo Grounds. It was early and she was alone, so he walked across, two bats in his hand, and leaned on the low rail.

"Didn't expect to see you here today, Maxine. Work slacking off?"

"No, Dad, not exactly. I had a free afternoon."

And it's Schoolboy Johnson pitching, he thought. Only she wouldn't, of course, be expected to admit this, so he said nothing.

She fooled him as she often had before. "Schoolboy is pitching today, and y'know, Dad, I've never seen him play."

Just think of it!

"Look, sister, this is none of my business and you know ballplayers a lot better than most, you ought to by this time; but my feeling is, this Johnson is bad medicine."

"So they tell me, Daddy. You're like everyone else; can't you see what's biting him?"

"No, I cannot. You got it figgered out?"

"Of course. The reason he loses his temper and blows is that he's frightened, and almost every time he pitches it makes him worse."

He stared at her. That young giant frightened? "Did you say he was frightened; did I get you correctly?"

"Certainly. That's it."

"With that fast ball of his, frightened? The boys who have to hit against him may be frightened—this lad Morris he hit last week could be—but Johnson, why should *he* be?"

"Don't you understand, he's new. He hasn't made the grade; he's not sure of himself. Remember how you were the first few weeks you came up?"

"Indeed I do, I remember I never went round telling old-timers like old Speedy they'd been up here too long for their own good. I never acted like a spoiled kid, never got the sulks when things didn't go right, never—"

"Naturally you didn't. You had confidence in yourself; he hasn't. Underneath he's terribly frightened, he's worried, that's why he won't learn a change-up, why he relies mostly on his fast ball. It's his best pitch so he uses it; makes him feel confident."

Roy Tucker looked down at his daughter. Was she pleading for the boy? "I still don't care for him. Neither do the rest of the boys on the club; even the bat boy don't go for him. And those kids are smart. As for the fellers on the other teams, a few like George Morris want to kill him. They would, too, if the chance came. If he's frightened, as you say, he takes a strange way of showing it."

Several women, one with a small youngster tagging along, entered the box. So he nodded and went out to the batting cage. Huh, frightened, he thought. First she claims he's cute. Six feet two, and cute! Now she says he's frightened. Women sure are funny.

That afternoon Schoolboy Johnson was great. His fast ball zoomed up to the plate, even giving Sunny Jim plenty of trouble—and the opposing batters a whole lot more. He seemed almost to dare the hitters; he used the curve sparingly, threw in the fast ball, not minding whether they knew most of the time what was coming. If they dug in, he let them, and burned the pitch past them.

Pop-ups, strike-outs, harmless grounders followed each other inning after inning. Up to the sixth, only two Giants, one on an error and one on a scratch hit, had reached first. Nobody got to second. The batters came to the plate; the batters returned to the dugout, shaking their heads in disgust.

One man tossed his stick away as he slumped to the bench after striking out for the third time. "Left-handers, right-handers, I've seen 'em all, but never anyone who threw harder than this guy."

The game became monotonous. People were even leaving the stands when George Morris came to bat in the sixth, with the Dodgers leading, 4-0. The Giant second baseman, a dead-end kid from East St. Louis, was a spunky little chap, full of fight and fire, like so many undersized men. He stood five feet five in his shower clogs and weighed a hundred and thirty-four pounds in a wet uniform on a day when the humidity was ninety per cent. Yet what he lacked in height and weight, he more than made up in pepper.

And he didn't care too much for Schoolboy Johnson.

George's nose had been broken in semi-pro boxing, and never repaired. He had one front tooth missing and he had never had it replaced. He was short, he was freckled, he was homely, he was a funny-looking runt. In fact, he was about everything Schoolie wasn't—or the other way round. So he disliked the tall, good-looking Dodger from the start. Then one day the week before, quite by accident, the Schoolboy had hit him square on his right forearm with a fast ball. George's dislike immediately turned to something deeper.

This afternoon he shoved close to the plate with a trace of bravado in his stance, as if daring the big pitcher to hit him again. It was a challenge the Schoolboy observed and accepted. On his second pitch, he threw deliberately close. The hitter spun round to avoid the ball, and was smacked solidly in the ribs. The blow sent him spinning to the ground.

He staggered at once to his feet, coughing, for his

breath was gone. Then, straightening up, he started for the mound, the stands watching silently. The contrast between the huge, tall pitcher and the pint-sized infielder was ludicrous; but his teammates knew him as a scrapper, so they swarmed from the dugout and yanked him to first base. There he died a moment later when the next batter flied out.

Still coughing and panting from the blow, he walked over as Schoolboy crossed the base path to the dugout.

"I . . . ever . . . get you . . . coming into second . . . Johnson . . . I'll cut you . . . to ribbons."

Schoolie stood still, hands on his hips. He looked down. "You wanna fight?" he asked suddenly.

The other was surprised but accepted immediately. "Yeah, yeah," he said eagerly, advancing with belligerence.

"O.K." replied the Schoolboy. He took several steps back, turned, and picked up the fifteen-year-old bat boy, Johnny O'Brien. Lifting him high in the air by his armpits, he tossed him in front of Morris. "O.K. then. Fight *him!*"

The crowd roared with delight. Though nobody had heard the verbal exchange, the affair had been acted out before their eyes, and it was quite impossible not to understand what had happened. Amusement swept the entire field. Life came into a rather dull contest. George Morris, more furious than ever, stood still while the bat boy picked himself up. Finally Morris turned and went slowly out to his position, laughter from the stands following every step.

Being funny at someone else's expense, with 40,000 fans watching, is a dangerous pastime. George Morris came to bat again in the ninth thirsting for trouble, fire in his gaze. Schoolboy knew that Stubblebeard, the plate umpire, would be watching closely, so he kept the ball well away from the batter. On the 2-2 count, George hit a short blooper back of second.

Shading his eyes, Bob Russell went back. Ed Peters, head in the air, charged out also, and Jackson Jones raced in. The ball dropped precisely between them, untouched.

From the moment it was hit, Schoolboy felt it would be a safety, and knew George Morris would try for two. Second base was open, so he ran over to cover it as Jackson grabbed up the ball and laced it into the bag. There he was, waiting in plenty of time, the ball carefully stuck in his glove as the batter slid in. He braced himself, expecting a shock, waiting to see those flashing spikes. Instead, a shower of dirt rose into his face, half blinding him. Then, with a quick move, George drew up one knee and kicked hard. And there was the ball rolling and bouncing along the grass back of second, Schoolie's glove near it.

Instantly Morris rose and lit out for third, shoving Schoolie, off balance and half blinded, from his path. He went down in the dirt as Morris raced for third, getting there easily before the ball was recovered.

Bruised, angry, disgusted, the Schoolboy picked the dirt from his eyes as the crowd yelled with pleasure. They cheered while he dusted off his uniform, they jeered with gusto and delight when he went over to take his glove from Ed. It was their first chance that afternoon to celebrate, and they made the most of it. From every corner of the park, voices assaulted him.

"Wise guy, huh?"

"See whatcha got, Johnson."

"You fresh busher!"

"How you like it, Johnson?"

True, the Dodgers were still leading, 4-0. But this incident brought solace to many a Giant heart.

Annoyed with himself, angry at what had happened, cursing the little Giant runner, with fingers still tingling from the blow, he turned grimly toward the box.

Before he got there, Roy Tucker, who missed nothing, ran over. "Hey, Schoolie, hurt bad?"

At first he didn't understand. Then he glanced down. In his chagrin and excitement, he had failed to notice the glove hanging from his fingers. It was covered with crimson. There was a gash across the back of his hand, from which blood was flowing freely.

Spike Russell reached the mound immediately, followed by the Doc, carrying his small black bag. The infield surrounded them, watching while the Doc swabbed the wound, poured some white powder on it to stop the bleeding, and bound it up with surgeon's plaster. The pitcher got his glove on, though with difficulty.

"Feel all right?"

"Sure I'm all right."

"If you're sure, then. Remember we want this one."

Spike and the Doc returned slowly to the bench. "Nothing but a slight cut; it looks worse than it is. Shouldn't bother him any," said the Doc reassuringly to the manager.

With Morris sitting in disdain on third base, the Schoolboy tossed in some pitches, the infield around him, watching. The fact was, the fall had shaken him badly; but with that pest on third he had no intention of leaving the game. His fast ball seemed full of zip, so the group around the mound dispersed slowly, the players returning to their positions, Spike and the Doc watching from the bench.

The next batter smacked a long, deep drive which High-pockets, with his back up against the fence, took for the second out. The fans rose expectantly, hoping it would go all the way, but although Morris scored easily, it was just another out, and the Schoolboy seemed to have the situation well in hand.

However, the following man got hold of a slant and hit it far over Jackson's head for two bases. A smart single brought him home; score 4-2.

From the corner of his eye, as he turned to finger the

rosin bag, Schoolboy Johnson saw the bull pen working with feverish haste. Shaken by the fall, his hand throbbing, upset by the two hits, he grew peevish when Sunny Jim called for the curve, and shook him off petulantly. His fast ball had won all day for him, so he bore in with everything he had. But a little edge was missing. The batter lofted it into the short left-field stands and the score was tied.

Spike came rushing out to the mound. He extended one hand for the ball. Schoolie turned his back, pretending not to see him as Spike waved toward the bull pen.

"I'm all right, Spike; let me stay in."

"Gimme the ball!"

"Naw, I'm all right, I tell ya. A game is nine innings; just let me pitch to this man."

"*Give me the ball.*"

Several players, among them Roy and Red, approached; but the Schoolboy kept the ball tight in his glove.

"Look, Schoolie, I said I wanted the ball. You understand English."

The big boy took off his glove, hurled it at his feet, and stamped on it.

A throaty roar of joy swept the stands. At this he tossed the ball over his head, and it rolled back of him toward second. Then he stalked from the mound, with the crowd openly jeering, and into the dugout, where he threw himself furiously down on the bench.

Roy Tucker hastily retrieved the ball and brought it over to Spike Russell.

Final score: Giants 7, Dodgers 4.

A game is nine innings.

CHAPTER 14

The Uses of Adversity

The buzz and hum in the stands continued after the game was over and the actors in the drama had vanished from sight. The fans were moving slowly toward the exits, discussing the end of the contest and the shellacking of Schoolboy Johnson, while the girl sitting in the front box listened to their comments as they passed.

"That Schoolie, he's a character all right. . . ."

"Too bad he's such a heel. . . ."

"Aw, it was time to yank him . . . more than time. . . ."

She sat in the box alone, in no hurry to leave. What was the hurry? Absolutely no hurry. So she stayed there, thinking, as the crowd thinned out. How, she wondered, do you handle this? He knows I'm here, waiting. It would take a wiser person than I am to know what to do next.

Naturally, she had no desire to see him, and her inclination was to let him alone. Moreover, she felt sure that in his misery and frustration of the moment he had no wish to see her or anyone else. Why not step quietly into her father's car in the parking lot and go home with him? It might be tactful. Then again, it might not.

Because that would seem like desertion. To anyone who knew baseball, the scene that she could picture in the clubhouse at the moment was not a pleasant one. The Schoolboy would be in the midst of them, surrounded by all those men, yet terribly alone, because none of them would have a word for him. If she walked out on him, that would be another blow.

Consequently, an hour later they were seated in a restaurant far out on Long Island. He drove all the way in silence, still numb from the humiliation and the punishment of that last inning. When food was put before him, he made an attempt to eat, but for once appetite had deserted him. So he sat there, the white bandage around his hand, eating nothing and saying nothing, completely subdued now, and intensely absorbed by his dejection.

"Eat something, Schoolie, try to eat a little."

"I don't wanna eat."

"But you must. You haven't had any food since breakfast."

"Don't feel like food now."

In a few minutes, though, he picked up his glass of milk and began to sip it, and soon he was morosely eating a few mouthfuls. At last he muttered, "Y'know, you're about the only one who isn't down on me. You understand baseball, you really know your baseball, not like some of these women. . . ."

She put her hand over his, on the table. For she did know a little, a tiny bit about baseball; it had been part of her existence as long as she could remember. She knew that baseball is really life in miniature: ups and downs, successes and failures, triumph and disappointment intermingled. How you met the failures and the disappointments showed the kind of person you were.

"Sweet are the uses of adversity." This she had discovered for herself as she watched her father over the years from the time she was a small child. You stumble and fall down; you pick yourself up and go on. What else can you do? You strike out with your team behind and the bases loaded in the ninth, or you go two for thirteen, so you arrive early at the empty ball park with the pitching coach the next morning, and make him throw to you for an hour or so. Not the fast balls you like, but the "junk stuff," the sliders and change-ups that have been fooling you.

Across the table the weary, heartsick boy mumbled something meaningless. He was, she perceived, a truly wretched soul, bruised by adversity. How would he meet it? How would he face the test everyone must meet sooner or later? This she wondered while he kept on grumbling, half to himself.

"Think he'd do that to Josh Crayton? Don't be funny. He would not; that guy is a twenty-five thousand dollar a year man, you gotta be nice to him. Would he do it to Speedy Mason? Naw, Speedy is a pal, an old-timer. Me, I'm a rookie. There's a difference."

She removed her hand hastily. A difference? Of course there's a difference; Spike Russell would never yank Speedy Mason so unceremoniously. Speedy learned his lesson years ago and wouldn't need that kind of treatment. Speedy doesn't throw at people's heads and get in messes as you do.

She started to suggest this, but realized in time it would only hurt him more and do no good whatever.

All the while he kept on mumbling. "Thinks he's a manager! Know what? Know what, Maxine? He's a sadist, that guy; likes to rub it in."

She frowned, trying to find some way to bring him to reality, to get him to face the situation as it existed, to make him see how his own conduct looked to outsiders, to the men on the bench, to the thousands in the stands, and especially to a girl in Box 56.

"Schoolie, tell me something. What did he say when he came to the mound that first time?"

"Whad' he say? The usual thing. They all say the same thing, these managers. Was I tired? Arm stiffening? Hurt bad? Did it bother me? As if he couldn't see the blood pouring down my hand like it was running from a hose! Him and that guy there that calls himself a trainer, that Doc. Don't tell me they couldn't see I **was** hurt; 'course they could see, same's everyone else."

"Yes, but. . . ." Now she was upset, and worried on his account also. She knew perfectly well he had insisted on staying in to finish the game. In fact, she understood what had happened almost as if she had been out in the little group around the mound when the Doc finished binding up his damaged hand. "Yes, but he needed this one, he wanted to win this one; if he'd felt you were badly hurt, if he saw you'd had it. . . ."

He didn't reply directly or at all. Instead he continued grumbling in an undertone. "That Russell! Calls himself a big-league manager; he couldn't manage a tank-town team in Texas for my money. Tell ya what, Maxine, truth is the guy's been up and around here in the majors far too long. The good managers are near enough the age of the players to understand their problems. Spike Russell has forgotten how he felt when he came up. The real managers are those fellers like Driberg of the Red Sox and Wagner of the Braves; they aren't so bossy. They can remember when they were players and some old crow was ridin' 'em for this and for that."

In his soreness and his sorrow he forgot momentarily he was talking to the daughter of Roy Tucker. Actually he forgot everything except those horrible moments of humiliation that afternoon. Ringing in his ears were the booing and the catcalls from the stands as he strode to the bench.

The girl sighed. As she sat listening to him condemn Spike Russell, the cause of all his misery, she realized the events of the afternoon had made no impression whatever upon him. He was still the stubborn, imperceptive young fathead, unable to see things objectively and accept blame for his own mistakes.

The more he complained, the more annoyed she became. The feeling of sympathy she had when they first sat down vanished. She let him have it.

"Schoolboy, look; remember the first time we met, when was it? A month—three weeks ago?"

That particular afternoon when he had discoursed at length about the man who happened to be her father was something he liked to forget, so he merely nodded.

"As I recall, you pitched a fine game that day and just missed a no-hitter with two out in the ninth. Right?"

"Yeah, yeah," he responded eagerly. For he enjoyed dwelling upon those moments in which he had come so close to fame. This was the first time since they had sat down when there was any animation in his expression. "Sure, I remember; except for that Ancient Mariner out there, that Karl Case in right field, I'da had a no-hitter. A no-hitter!" His voice took on that tone it had the afternoon when he leaned over the window of her father's car. "I won it, I earned it, then that clown. . . ."

"Yes, that was Case's fault; he spoiled your no-hitter."

"I'll say," he replied with enthusiasm, attacking his food vigorously. "Yep, you're dead right, he cost me that one. And let me tell you, there's another guy too old . . . over the hill."

She kept on boring in. "Then this George Morris, he spiked you at second base and ruined your throwing the rest of the inning, didn't he?"

"Aw, sure, he got away with it; hadda been a decent umpire, not that Catfish Simpson out there, that blind man back of second. . . . Yeah, he got away with it; believe me, he won't again. Next time Morris comes to bat and I'm throwing, he better watch out, that's all; he better duck, and fast."

"Yes, the accident, and the spiking, and the injury to your hand, that was all Morris's fault."

Suspiciously he turned upon her. What was she getting at? "Well, you sat right there, you saw the whole thing, you watched the guy come riding in with his spikes high."

"Yes, I saw it all. But then again, he had nothing to do with your actually finishing the game."

"Oh, no, that was up to Spike Russell, he manages the team, he yanked me. Though just between you and me, where that Russell would be without Fat Stuff and the coaches, I dunno."

"Maybe you've got something there. Anyhow, the point is, you lost your no-hitter through the fault of Karl Case. You got injured because of Morris. Your having to come out of the game was due to Russell; he's the manager, as you say. Let's look at this a minute. First it was Case, then Morris, then Russell. But Schoolie, you know you do have some responsibility for what happened, yourself."

Silence. Not a word out of him. He laid down his

fork and stared at her. A small stain of red had penetrated the bandage on his hand. It stood out upon the white gauze. For a moment he seemed about to speak, to burst into words. Then, with an effort, he held himself in.

She could see what a strain he was under. At last he said, despairingly, "I getcha. You're like all the rest. I had you figured different; but you're against me too."

This was more than she could take. Her affection disappeared; she wasn't even sorry for him any more. On the contrary, she was disgusted with his childishness and his petulance. "Look, once I saw my father out there in center field with a gangrened leg he couldn't stand on. Only he did, for nine innings, because they needed him; there wasn't anyone else to put in center field. Errors? Sure he made errors, but he didn't blame them on his leg, or on the manager, either. He took what was coming. You didn't. Until you learn to, you'll never be a ball-player."

He flushed under the coat of tan, rose, sat down. "What d'you mean I can't take it? What d'you know about baseball, you never played. I really been through it . . . came up the hard way, from the minors. . . ."

"I mean just what I said—you can't take it. You're still a great big kid, blaming everyone else but yourself for your own mistakes. Why not grow up? It's about time."

He rose again, tossing his napkin to the table.

"I'm leaving, sister."

She sat there looking up at him. "Can't be too soon for me."

He turned, walked across to the door, where the head-waiter was standing beside a kind of high desk. Everyone in the room turned at the sight of the big blond boy with the red-spotted bandage wrapped around his hand. Several men leaned over to whisper, and she knew what they were all saying.

"That's Schoolboy Johnson of the Dodgers. He was knocked out today in the. . . ."

He hauled out two bills, peered down at the check, handed the money to the headwaiter, and turned away, stuffing his wallet in his hip pocket.

She watched his familiar golden thatch as it disappeared from the room. The outer door of the restaurant shut. Soon a motor whirred in the parking lot outside, and a car roared out into the highway. Maxine Tucker sat alone at the little table in the corner of the air-conditioned restaurant.

She was not thinking of herself, or how she could manage to get home. She was thinking of Schoolboy Johnson and how easy it was for a man to ruin his career. He's got to grow up, that's certain.

Kings, presidents, baseball managers, even Schoolboy Johnson, the same as everyone else.

CHAPTER 15

Bean Ball

The National League was still a grand old free-for-all in the first part of September. But like the brisk nights of fall, it had cooled off slightly. The Braves' lead over the Dodgers was now three and a half games instead of two. Far from gaining, the Dodgers were losing ground. Moreover, a western trip loomed ahead, and little time was left.

Spike Russell consequently wasn't the happiest man in baseball. Cassidy, his best pitcher, was still in the hospital, recovering from that automobile accident. Josh Crayton, the great hurler, the stopper and the most dependable man on the staff, was tired from the heat and the double-headers piling up. Schoolboy Johnson seemed invincible to a point, and usually went to pieces in the late innings. Following that shellacking by the Giants, he grew sullen, more of a loner than ever. Speedy Mason's arm was worn down. As for the overworked bull-pen pitchers, they were creaking at the seams.

That wasn't the worst. Red Allen had played three months without missing a game, day or night, Sundays and holidays, single ones and double-headers. Sunny Jim's left hand was in such bad shape it prevented him from gripping his bat firmly. Worst of all was that lengthening lead. So Spike was in a poor mood as they opened a double-header against the Cubs, the last series before the final western trip of the year.

He nodded curtly as Casey sauntered over to the bench before the game. For a while he said nothing, but when the sports writer murmured something about things being tough, Spike opened up.

"Tough? I'll say. This is the time a feller earns his pay. A manager's job is so easy when the hitters are powdering the ball and the pitchers find the plate; it's when everything goes wrong that you can't sleep nights. Tell ya, Casey, what a guy needs at times like these is patience. You want to rip things apart, you want to do something. It really hurts to sit here and do nothing. But if you've got a sound ball club, that's the only way out. You have to have patience, to remember the guys feel just as bad as you do."

"Yeah, I've noticed the managers who stay cool get the best results. See where you've got the Schoolie in action again."

"Uh-huh, hand looked worse'n it was. He won't pitch today; but he could. It healed real quick."

"Has he learned anything, Spike?"

"Most likely not. 'Cept never to tangle with that boy Morris again."

"Morris," remarked Casey, lighting a cigarette. "Isn't he something!"

"Yeah," said the manager unenthusiastically.

"I recall the year he came up. I was covering the Giants that season. First game they played in Pittsburgh, old Sutherland, the southpaw, smacked George square on the noggin. George got up, didn't say a word, just trotted to first. When the inning was over, he said to one of the coaches, 'All right, if it's that kind of a league, I'll play it that way.' Later in the game he made a hit, and went for second. He slid into the bag and broke both the short-stop's kneecaps. Put him out for the rest of the season."

"Yeah, and of all people, that man Morris is the one Johnson has to pick on."

Big Red Allen came toward them with a bat in one hand and slumped wearily to the bench. His face was wet with sweat; he yanked off his cap and pulled his sleeve across his forehead. "Hotting up again."

Spike said nothing, so Casey answered, "Sure is; hotter'n blazes." He noticed the drawn lines about the player's mouth, his face tight with fatigue. "How ya feel, Red?"

The first baseman looked at him quickly. "Feel? Fine, fine. Only I'm not getting my base hits."

Nor was he the only one. The club was in a batting slump. Nothing broke right for the Dodgers. Liners screamed into the gloves of waiting outfielders, balls took

the wrong bounce, every decision went against them.
They were behind in the second, equaled the Cubs with
two runs in the fourth, fell behind in the sixth. The
Dodger bull pen was as busy as the vendors selling cold
drinks in the stands, and one by one the pitchers wilted.

In the last of the ninth, they came to bat two runs
behind, three outs from defeat by a last-place club. Jackson Jones, the first batter, worked the pitcher for a pass.
Roy Tucker, next up, got the count to 3-2. He stepped
from the box and turned toward third for the sign.

The fastest runner in the club was on base and the
hitter a man who could punch the ball to right. So Spike,
desperate, gambled and ordered the hit and run.

Meanwhile, in the living room of a ranch house out on
Long Island, a girl leaned toward a television set. She
watched her father's familiar gesture as she had hundreds
of times before, saw him lean over, rub dirt on his hands,
wipe them on the side of his pants, and step in. Then he
touched the rim of his cap to indicate he had the signal.
Arms outstretched, Jackson Jones on the base path near
first returned the signal too.

The pitcher looked toward the bag, went into his set
position, and threw. Roy connected.

It was a long, low liner that sailed above the second
baseman's glove as he leaped in the air—a perfectly timed
hit that drew an instant roar of appreciation from the
crowd, because it seemed likely to go to the fences for
extra bases. Jackson was off the minute the ball had left

the pitcher's hand. He tore around second and started for third. But the Cub right fielder, jumping high, stopped the ball on the bounce, cut it off, and prevented its going through. Jackson was lucky to get into third safely.

The gamble had paid off. There were men on first and third with nobody out. All over the field came the crowd roar from the stands, the rising, insistent call for a hit, the cheers and shouts and the high-pitched yells from the bleacher kids packed in the second tier.

Sunny Jim Carter stood in the circle. He was in a fearful batting slump caused by his bruised hand, and for a moment Spike considered a pinch hitter. He glanced up and down the bench. There was nobody available; he had used up his three pinch hitters during the game, so he was forced to go with his injured catcher.

The stands kept yelling for a hit. They screamed, pleaded, stomped, yelled. And they quieted down quickly, too, as the pitcher went ahead of the batter—two strikes and a ball. The noise died away completely as Sunny Jim hit a slow roller toward first. The fielder charged it, took the ball, arm back, ready to gun it to the plate. But Jackson, making a feint, returned quickly to third, so the fielder stepped over and tagged the catcher as he raced by.

Now came the pitcher's turn. Once again Spike Russell glanced up and down the long bench. What about the Schoolboy? Why not? After all, he's hitting .309.

"Schoolie! Get up there for Stetson. Bring that man home."

The boy went to the bat rack, took his club, and stepped from the dugout. The crowd cheered, and there were some boos mixed in with the cheers, too.

In that living room on Long Island, the girl caught the voice of the announcer, and the yell that followed.

"Johnson . . . number 58 . . . batting for Stetson."

What she could not hear was the grim comment Spike Russell made to the man sitting beside him.

"If he can't pitch, at least he can hit."

"Loves to hit."

"What pitcher doesn't?"

"No, but Schoolboy really loves to. See how loose he is up there."

Indeed he was loose, deceptively so. To everyone who watched, especially to that girl out on Long Island, he seemed free and easy. If he manages to bring those men across, she thought, he'll make up for an awful lot with Spike Russell.

There he stood, waggling his bat carelessly, completely relaxed. The pitcher glanced mechanically toward third, and threw.

At the plate the boy turned and tried to duck.

"Oh!" shrieked the girl. "Oh!" She watched as the batter went down, grabbing at his head.

CHAPTER 16

No Visitors

A little sign hung on the outer handle of the door: *No Visitors.*

Inside, the room was darkened and quiet, the shades drawn. The blond head lay against the white pillow, motionless, a damp cloth over the forehead and eyes. In the feeble ray cast by the dim light over the back of the bed, a homely, stoutish nurse was trying to read the sports pages of the *Daily News.* Her tone was low, casual, as if she were reading about someone neither of them had ever seen.

"In the ninth, Schoolboy Johnson, pinch-hitting for Stetson, the hurler, got smacked on the head by one of Dave Hanlon's fast balls. He was apparently unable to duck or shift his feet at the last moment. He was removed on a stretcher and taken to Presbyterian Hospital, where he passed a restless night."

So that's what they call a restless night! With an angry

gesture he chucked the damp cloth from his forehead and tried to lift himself up. A pain went down the back of his neck, sharp, intense, and he collapsed immediately onto the pillow.

"There, you see what the doctor told you; you mustn't move, you're to lie still. See what happens? Here, let me put that back." She replaced the damp cloth over his eyes.

"These sports writers, what do they know anyhow? Guy chucks a bean ball at your noggin, and they claim your feet are locked. Right at me, nurse, right straight at my head."

"Yes, well you relax now and take it easy, Mr. Johnson. You'll get well much quicker that way; you want to get well as soon as possible, don't you? Of course. And whatever happens, don't make a sudden move like that. It's dangerous."

She folded the newspaper, felt his damp forehead, and, closing the door quietly, left the room. Perhaps what hurt Schoolie as much as anything was the term, "restless night."

I wish they'd had the pains and the terrible headache I had all night; they wouldn't call it restless.

About two hours later there was a tap on the door and the doctor entered, his hands full of X rays. The man in the white coat said good morning, sat down in the chair beside the bed, and began talking. His voice was low, but his tone was cheerful.

"We have the X rays now, and I'm very happy to say

there are no complications: no concussion, no fractures, so far as we can tell. Everything seems quite normal; but of course you realize you've received a bad blow, Mr. Johnson, and you'll need a little time to get over it. For the next few days, rest, quiet, isolation. Mustn't see anyone or move around."

He rose, holding an X ray up to the dim light above the bed. Then he held up another and another. There were eight in all. For a long while he concentrated upon them, saying nothing. Schoolie did not feel like talking either; it even hurt to talk, and the pills they had given him did not stop that racking headache.

Finally the boy in the bed spoke. "Head hurts."

The doctor accepted this information as doctors always do, with little interest. "H'm . . ." he said, still holding the X rays up to the light. "Yes, it will, no doubt, for some time; you must expect that. In fact, all your life you'll probably have a slight headache in damp weather. Son, let me tell you you're a mighty fortunate young man. You came as near to death—or something worse—as anyone can. An inch lower and you'd have had it. H'm."

He kept inspecting the X rays and holding them up to the light as he talked. "Like Billy Rogers of the Yankees. I had him three years ago and he's never played baseball since. Never will, can't even hold down a steady job. One inch lower, and you'd have been in his shoes. So consider yourself the luckiest man in the major leagues."

"I do, doctor, only when do you think. . . ."

"When will you be playing again? Everyone asks the same question. If you behave, if you stay still, don't move around or get excited or try to see people for a few days, you'll be out the end of the week. It's up to you. And don't forget how lucky you've been."

He shuffled up his X rays, nodded, and went out. The door shut silently. For the next two painful days and nights, and for the first time in his life, Schoolboy Johnson was alone in the dark with his thoughts. In the midst of that unceasing agony he lay alone thinking, because it was all he could do. Perhaps it was the first time in his life he had ever seriously thought.

To be nudged by death is a sobering experience. To the Schoolboy it was new, frightening. He was shaken up. There was a lot to think about, especially the past few weeks since he had come up to the Dodgers. As he reflected upon them, an unpleasant idea struck him suddenly. It came in the middle of a sleepless night when unpleasant ideas always come. It was still with him when he woke from a troubled dream the next morning, and it stayed with him through the long day, persisted, invaded his consciousness, though he tried to forget it, to shove it away.

Could that girl have been right?

The scene in the clubhouse kept returning to him. Stretched on the rubbing table, he looked up to see the Cub pitcher standing over him, silent, wide-eyed, and frightened. And he remembered his own tempestuous outburst with no pleasure.

"You . . . you son of a sea cook, Hanlon . . . call yourself a pitcher . . . throwing at a man's head like that, just because you're scared of him. You so-and-so . . . you. . . ."

Yet could it be possible that all this was, well, not my fault exactly, but on *me?* For my feet *were* locked; I remember I tried hard to duck and couldn't. That's a fact. It *was* my fault; I had it coming to me.

It's all very confusing. Let's see, suppose Case, that time, wasn't playing right for the batter in the ninth, or suppose, just for an argument, that the guy crossed him up and hit to the wrong field. Then it wasn't his fault at all that I lost my no-hitter. No . . . it . . . really wasn't, was it?

Wryly and with regret he recalled how Karl Case had come over to his locker after the game to say he was sorry, and his own contemptuous brush-off. To Case, the man who had been patrolling right field for sixteen years, who never argued with umpires or squawked, or got into fights, or made the usual mistakes. Case, the old pro. Just suppose it wasn't Karl's fault, after all.

Then maybe I riled George Morris up that afternoon by chucking the bat boy at him. That was funny, it was pretty darned funny at the time; but it made him look like a fool. I can see that now. I realize he naturally wanted to get at me; he's not the type to take that sort of thing lying down. So possibly my being spiked was my own

fault. Maybe I had it . . . could be I had it coming to me.
His head ached and now something else hurt worse. If
that girl was right that evening, and these things were my
fault and not someone else's, what kind of a heel was I to
walk away and leave her in a restaurant miles from home?
The only person who was *for* me, who understood, who
knew baseball and knew me. What did I do it for?

These were some of the things he turned over in his
mind as he lay alone in that darkened room. On the morning of the third day something happened entirely by
chance. He was much better that morning; the throbbing
pain in his forehead had diminished, the bump was re-
duced, the dizziness gone. This happened to be the moment the cleaner chose to polish the doorknobs of every
room along the fifth-floor corridor. He removed the *No
Visitors* sign from Schoolie's room, and neglected to re-
place it.

Consequently, when Speedy Mason was told at the main
office, by some careless attendant, that a Mr. Johnson was
in room 506 on the fifth floor, he went up in the elevator,
passed a cloud of chattering nurses in a glass-enclosed
cubbyhole, knocked feebly on number 506, and, in response to an answer, went in.

"Who's that?" asked the Schoolboy, looking up, the
bandage having been removed.

"It's me, Speedy Mason." The visitor was slightly awed
by the darkened room and the figure in the bed.

"Oh," the Schoolboy answered, assuming the doctor had

given permission for him to have visitors. "Oh . . . sit down, Speedy. Nice of you to come. Glad to see you."

He *was* glad, too. For he found himself rather dismal company, and the fat nurse was no help at all. To Spike he would, perhaps, have talked more freely; but he needed to talk, to say things to someone on the club who knew him well, to get out some of the things he had been thinking.

And Speedy Mason knew him pretty well, after all.

"How ya doing, Schoolie, old boy? Be back soon, I hope. We can sure use ya. This is our last game on the home stand tonight; tomorrow we leave for the West. When d'you expect they'll spring you?"

"End of the week, the doc said, if everything goes all right. I'll be glad to get out; believe me, this is no fun. Say, Speedy, maybe it's a good thing you came along. I've been thinking a lot these past few days here alone, and I'm beginning to see some things more clearly. Get me?"

The other man looked at him curiously. Was it possible Dave Hanlon's fast ball had knocked some sense into this crazy kid? Or had the blow affected his mind? It did, occasionally. Speedy Mason recalled Jerry Kates of the White Sox and Ken Stafford of the Cards and several others who had never been the same after a beaning.

So he replied noncommittally. "Yeah . . . tha's so, Schoolboy?"

"Uh-huh. Look, Speedy, I want to be a pitcher."

"Why, Schoolie, whaddya mean, you *are* a pitcher, and

a good one. Don't let one crack on the head upset you."

He interrupted. "No, I'm not; I know I'm not. I'm a long ways from being a pitcher and it took this shaking up and these days here alone to make me see it. I never knew what it was to be conked by a fast ball; believe me, Speedy, I do now. I want to be a pitcher. Not someone who blows at the end of a game; but a real, strong, consistent, nine-inning thrower, as good with the last man as the first. Like you are."

Yep, he's nuts, definitely nuts, thought Speedy. This couldn't be the surly kid who threw things around the room because he couldn't stay out late with that girl in Milwaukee? Or the Schoolie who came up last month— I'm good, I know I'm good, and where do you get off? That was his attitude. Can't believe he means what he's just been saying.

There was silence as Speedy Mason did some thinking. Or has this crazy screwball got some sense at last? Has he come to realize pitching is a test of skill, of nerves, of character? If so, there's hope for him, and for the club, too.

"Well, Schoolie, I b'lieve I'll take you at your word. You want to be a pitcher, a good pitcher, a top-class man. That's a big order. You're a real fine thrower right now, you got the fastest pitch in the league, most everyone is scared of you. But that isn't all there is to pitching, and, like you say, I gotta admit you really aren't a pitcher yet. Now, if you're serious. . . ."

"I sure am, Speedy."

He looked it, intense, earnest, frowning from the high hospital bed and staring down at the man beside him.

"Good. First-off, you got to perfect your change-up. It's no good. You been busting the ball past the hitters, but you can't go on that way. Fat Stuff can teach you a real change-up in a few hours; so could I. Then comes the hard part, the reason so many pitchers never master it, the practice, lots of practice, hour after hour, morning after morning, until you have it under control. See now, the guys are waiting until the last innings when maybe your fast ball has lost a tiny bit of zip and zing; they dig in and meet it. Some of 'em are bound to connect."

"Consider it settled. I'll learn a real good change-up and, believe me, I won't be satisfied until I throw it as well as you do. Day I get back I'll go to work with you. Then what?"

The old pitcher shifted uneasily in his chair. Now comes the difficult thing to say. Shall I let him have it straight, is he able to handle this, how will he take it? Maybe he'll explode and kick me out of the room. "Then what?" He tried hard to sound casual. "Oh . . . then . . . it's up to you."

"Yes . . . but how do you mean?"

"Schoolie, pitching is all one thing—how you meet the tough situations. That's easy enough the first few innings when a man is fresh and the hitters go down one-two-three; but toward the end, when you're bushed and beaten, when your fielders make bobbles or throw to the wrong bag or do something silly 'cause they're tired and not thinking well, then this is tough. So you learn to control yourself, to keep your concentration. Forget the last man. Concentrate on the batter. Forget that error in the field that may cost a run; put out a little extra. Every good pitcher must—and does. See what I mean? It's a kind of test."

"I see. Test of a guy."

"Test of a guy's character. That's about all baseball is, a test of character, how you react under pressure, when things go wrong, when you're behind and. . . ."

"I getcha. Never thought about it this way. Speedy, up here alone I've had some time these past few days to go back . . . to go over . . . well, to see a few mistakes I made."

"Aw, forget it, boy. We all make 'em; I did at your age. Oh, yes, I did. So did Josh Crayton; why one time he was a national choke-up."

"Not like me."

"Worse! Come back and work, show 'em that change-up, don't depend on your fast ball so much, mix up your pitches. Get out and throw that ball and have some fun, Schoolie, get some fun out of the game. Why, you haven't had any fun since you came up; you've been in trouble. . . ."

"I'll say. I realize it, too. But it's my fault."

Now Speedy Mason was staggered. *His* fault? Look

who's talking! That beaning must have taught him a lesson. His fault! What a pitcher he can be if he means it!

"Oh . . . one more thing. Quit worrying. A good pitcher must stop worrying about his pitching; if he doesn't, he's through. They'll try their best to upset you, to tease you; they know if they can they'll win. If they don't, you win. Every club in the league right now thinks they have your number. Here's your chance to show how wrong they are. It's up to you."

The door opened abruptly and the fat nurse stood there with a tray on which were two white pills and a glass of water.

She stopped, her mouth open. "*Mr. Johnson!* You aren't supposed to have visitors yet! Who let this gentleman in?" She turned quickly. "And who took the sign off the doorknob?"

CHAPTER 17

Only a Base on Balls

It was a dampish night with a cold fall wind blowing off Lake Michigan over County Stadium. There were only nine games left, and the Dodgers, still three behind, had split the first two contests of their series with the Western clubs. This, the final battle with Milwaukee, would not mean the pennant if they won, because they would still be two games behind with eight to go. But if they lost it, the Braves were in.

Casey, the sports writer, was sitting on the bench of the home team, talking to the Milwaukee manager.

"They want to win bad, those boys," the manager said. "That Mason, him and the Schoolboy and their pitching coach were working out all morning."

"No! That right?" said Casey, wondering to himself.

"They'll never make a pitcher out of that kid; he's a strike thrower, not a corner thrower like Speedy Mason.

Why, yesterday afternoon the old-timer was getting the littlest part of the plate with his curve, had our boys all buffaloed. And that humpbacked let-up pitch he tosses— that's a teaser."

Casey glanced across the field, where the Schoolboy was chucking steadily to a bull-pen catcher. "Well, I'd say pitching is one thing *you* don't have to worry about. Spike Russell would like to have your troubles."

"Yep, our pitchers are mostly sound, thank goodness. I guess you have to admit the situation is in our favor. But shucks, we could still lose; we aren't spending the dough yet." Like all managers, he played it cautiously.

Casey had to agree. "They're tough still, but they're dog-tired and, as you say, the situation is all your way. Three games ahead and nine left. Nice spot to be in."

"Yes, but then again, this team of Russell's are old, some of them, yet they have some mighty good ballplayers just the same. Now you take that Tucker; there's a man I hate to see coming to the plate when things are bad. He may be forty, but how he can run! And he's still the best fadeaway slider in the National League."

"Uh-huh, but he hits no homers these days."

"Maybe not. But he beats you in so many different ways."

The Dodgers were indeed an ancient, battle-weary club. Yet they were not beaten. Whenever one man went into a slump, another took up the slack. All through this final western trip it had been Roy Tucker lifting them in the tight games, delivering the clutch hit, making the stop with men aboard to save the pitcher. It was as if he couldn't forget that missed signal back in Brooklyn had cost them a vital game which would have made them only two games out of first place, instead of three.

It was the Schoolboy's first day back with the club, and the players straggling onto the field before the game shook hands with him, asked how he felt, and stood watching as he kept chucking to the catcher, Fat Stuff at his side. Before the game he went into the clubhouse, changed into a dry uniform, and, wrapped in his jacket, a towel muffling his neck, sat beside Speedy Mason in the middle of the bench.

Big Josh Crayton was at his best tonight against this team of sluggers, and had to be. For the first four scoreless innings each pitcher dominated the hitters. Then Josh got careless; a batter teed off on his fast ball, hitting a homer into the stands and putting the Braves ahead, 1-0. Josh then bore down and struck out the next three men.

But in the last of the sixth there were men on first and second with nobody out. The next batter popped to Red Allen. Then with one down, a man mistimed a pitch and struck a slow, high bounder to the pitcher's right. Ed Peters charged in, but suddenly, from nowhere, Roy ran across in front of him. He had sized up the play and knew their only chance of nailing the hitter was to cut the ball off and fire it fast to Red. So he raced over, leaped up, speared it on the run, and rifled a throw to the bag a step ahead of the runner. If it had gone through to short, the man would have been safe and the bases loaded. Josh got the next batter to fly to Highpockets and they were out of a tight inning.

In the seventh, the Dodgers opened with a ringing single by Karl Case. Red Allen was ordered to hit away, and when Roy walked over for his bat, Spike leaned toward him and spoke quietly.

"If Red goes down, bunt that man along to second, Roy."

Red hit the ball well, a liner to center; but the outfielder snagged it and there was one out. As Roy stepped in, the Braves' infield came alive for the bunt, racing in on each pitch, the first and third basemen crowding the plate, the second baseman covering first. Roy waved his stick, waiting until the 2-1 count for the ball he wanted. Then he pushed a smart bunt past the pitcher and right into the territory left vacant by the second baseman. Karl tore around second for third.

On the bench, the Schoolboy heard Spike's tone of admiration.

"Looka that Tucker! Look at him! If I told him to go up there and get hit on the head, by ginger, he'd do it. Ouch . . . watch yourself, Karl . . . watch it . . . watch it. . . ."

The coach had waved him on, but the Braves' right fielder, coming in fast, grabbed the ball and threw a strike to third. The man on the bag put the tag on Karl, turned, and saw Roy steaming for second, so without hesitation he drew back and threw to cut him down.

His hurried throw was high and over the shortstop's glove. Roy kept moving around second and headed for third as the ball bobbled and bounced along the grass, the same distance from both fielders. The coach behind third gave Roy the green light, and in a cloud of dust he scuttled for home. Ball and runner reached the plate together, but with a hooked slide he evaded the catcher's tag, and the score was tied.

So the two teams came into the ninth even. There were two out and the bases empty when Roy again stepped to the plate. After fouling off half a dozen pitches, he finally worked a base on balls.

"A base on balls," murmured Speedy. "A base on balls doesn't count so much with two down. Not good right here."

"Think he'll send him down?" asked the Schoolboy.

"He's entirely on his own. Has been all through this trip. Watch him out there."

Roy was taking a sizable lead, dancing and prancing off first, sliding headfirst back again to the bag, shaking off the dirt, and darting out again, edging toward second, farther, farther, retreating fast while the man in the box threw in, keeping a watchful eye on his movements. He tossed a pitch-out to the plate, but Roy wasn't biting. Once again he repeated his quick darts and feints, drawing throw after throw.

Then he was off.

With a good jump on the pitcher, he had no trouble sliding in safely at second. Now the stands were uneasy. They realized, as the pitcher did, that the base runner was dangerous. From the bench the Dodgers called to Sunny Jim for a hit.

Schoolie, his head aching from the dampness, just as the doctor had predicted, watched Roy go into his act again, moving toward third in tiny, catlike jumps, sliding back on his belly as he drew a quick throw from the pitcher. And another. And another. The whole park now concentrated upon this duel between the man on base and the man on the mound—none more intently than Schoolboy Johnson. This, he perceived, is what the old pitcher meant when he talked of pitching as a test of character. This is the final, ultimate test, here in the ninth, with the pennant hanging on the skill and courage of two men. Who will crack first?

Then, apparently on orders, Jim was passed to set up a play at first base, and Josh Crayton, a good hitting pitcher, lumbered to the plate. Over by second, Roy danced around, charging toward third on each throw, hoping to draw an error. But the Braves' catcher was playing it conservatively. Calling time, he walked to the mound. He and the pitcher stood with their heads together. Then they broke it up and the catcher returned to his place.

Once more Roy defiantly took a lead down the base path. The pitcher could hear his spikes grinding the dirt; he glanced back but did not risk a throw. Instead, he pitched wide. The catcher stepped out and burned the ball to second.

Roy had timed his maneuver perfectly. As the catcher's arm went back, he was off. The shortstop's throw to third was hurried and high, so, in a terrific cloud of dust, Roy reached out, pawing for the bag.

Now the advantage was his. He seemed to own the bases. Everyone was watching him, and from the bench Schoolie had the feeling that Roy was alone on the field. He did as he pleased, he was perpetual motion, and his antics obviously bothered the pitcher. Try as he would, the man on the mound could not help hearing those spikes scraping the dirt, and Roy's sudden stops and turns, and the yells of the coaches, and the cries from the Dodger bench.

"Look out. . . ."

"Watch him . . . he's going. . . ."

"Watch him . . . look out . . . look out. . . ."

The Schoolboy turned to Speedy. "Think he'll come all the way?"

"Not him. He's merely trying to upset the pitcher, to make the guy wonder if he will. Guess he's succeeding, too. If you're worrying about a base runner, you aren't thinking about your next pitch."

He was right. The pitcher lost Josh Crayton, filling the bases and bringing Bobby Russell to the plate. The Milwaukee manager stalked out, held a conference at the mound, returned to the bench.

Schoolie recalled the words of the veteran pitcher, spoken in the hospital room: "It's how you react under pressure."

There it all was before his eyes, the eternal drama of the pitcher and the base runner, and this time the pennant was at stake. The pressure was on each, and especially, now that the bases were filled, on the Braves' pitcher. The Schoolie observed Roy grow bolder and bolder, racing at full speed for the plate on every pitch, as if daring the man in the box, or the catcher, to throw. Neither accepted his offer. So he dashed back and forth as he pleased, the pitcher twice throwing wide of the plate, balls that would have nailed him had he been coming all the way.

But this was not the time to waste pitches. Slowly pressure told. Bobby Russell watched the two pitch-outs, fouled a strike over the corner, took a high one, while from third, Roy charged in each time as if he would surely try to steal. Then came a roar. The next pitch was a ball and Bobby flung his bat away. Only a base on balls— but it meant the tie was broken. It might also mean the pennant.

Halfway to home when the pitch was called, Roy eased

up and trotted across the run. Even the Milwaukee stands gave him an ovation, and the Dodger bench welcomed him with the greetings they usually reserved for a grand-slam homer. Ten minutes later they left the field, only two games behind.

CHAPTER 18

Only One Out to Go

Josh Crayton sat on the bench before his locker, sweating. Although most of the boys were still suiting up, he had finished his daily stint. The day after pitching, he simply ran to keep his legs in shape—twenty-five laps around the park. There he sat, mopping his face with a towel, as he read Casey's column in the *Mail*.

"Hey, you guys, see what that Casey had to say about my game yesterday? He says: 'Josh coasted along until the fifth.' How do you like that? Me straining my guts on every pitch, and he calls that 'coasting along!'"

It was five days after his victory over Milwaukee, won thanks to his fine pitching, to Roy Tucker on the bases, and a little luck. On the following day there had been another well-pitched victory. The Dodgers, with four games to go, were only one behind the leaders, so Spike was using his most dependable pair as often as he could: Crayton and Mason, Crayton and Mason, with only a few days' rest in between.

A wild pitch, a bad bounce, a bobble in the field could cost the pennant. Therefore he took no chances. Once he had tossed in the Schoolboy to relieve in the late innings and got away with it, but he preferred to stay with his reliable hurlers. This afternoon he was going again with Speedy Mason.

On the field, a little later, Fat Stuff stood beside the Schoolboy, his arms folded. They were watching the old pitcher warm up in front of them.

"Notice him carefully; so many youngsters tend to throw too much before a game—and too hard. Why, I was watching this young firebrand over in Philadelphia the other day, this Washburn White. He must have tossed in thirty pitches, real hard. Result: he had nothing left in the eighth, absolutely nothing. That's silly. You're only giving away stuff you could use later in the game when you do that."

"Yes, I see, I getcha. He's throwing easy, just a little loosening up, huh?"

"Why sure he is, just throwing to loosen up his arm; he'll only chuck in a few hard ones to finish off."

That afternoon Speedy Mason was sharp. In fact, he seemed better for only three days' rest. He cut the corners with his curve and snapped off his change-up. The team, as always when he was in the box, backed him up magnificently; they played with confidence. They gave him a lead early when Highpockets doubled and Karl brought him home with a single over second. Then Red Allen lifted one into the upper deck of the left-field stands.

The big first baseman ran quickly around the bases, in a kind of inconspicuous manner, running through the reception committee at the plate, hardly touching his cap in response to the yells and screams from above as he neared the dugout. It was almost as if he disliked hitting homers.

The game went on rapidly. In the box, Speedy was all business, going after the hitters with aggression, polishing them off with his curve and his slider. It was 3-0 going into the fifth when six runs made by the Braves against the Cards went up on the scoreboard in right. Speedy was good; he had to be.

Mickey Forbes, the third-base coach, slumped down on the bench beside the Schoolboy in the sixth as Speedy took the mound. Already the fever of excitement ran round the stands, swept into the distant bleachers in center, communicated itself to the benches, even to the players themselves. For the veteran hadn't yet given up a hit.

"Man, he's really got it today," said the Schoolboy. "Keeps on this way, he'll have something to cheer about."

"You said it. He's pacing himself, too. Those sweeping curves don't take it out of a pitcher like fast balls. . . . Look out! Watch him, big boy, you'll lose this man."

On the 3-1 pitch the curve missed the corner by an inch, and the first Philadelphia runner was on. A left-handed power hitter came to the plate.

Often someone in the infield would run across to the

mound to make a suggestion to the hurler—but not today. Even Red Allen, who habitually reminded the pitcher to cover first when a left-handed batter came up, refrained. Nobody presumed to tell the veteran how to play ball.

Standing astride the rubber, legs apart, the old-timer yanked at the peak of his cap. His glove hung by its strap from his wrist as he massaged the ball thoughtfully. Then, leaning over, he shook off Sunny Jim. He stepped on the rubber, glaring at first, and, without any windup, threw.

The batter connected—a low, vicious drive just beyond first. Ordinarily Red would have been there to field it; but he was holding the runner tight on the bag, and the ball appeared to be headed for extra bases.

Schoolboy bent forward, watching. In a flash Red was back there, his glove was out, he scooped it off the ground, almost tumbling into the dirt. Off balance, he had to stop, pivot, and race for the bag. Then he whirled to Ed Peters, who had hustled over to cover second as Red fielded the ball, and tossed it to him on a string. It was a double play and now the pressure was off the old pitcher.

The next batter hit a lazy, high fly to center. Jackson Jones drifted gracefully under it. In the box, Speedy spun round and watched Jackson, in center, slap his glove several times; then, without waiting, he turned his back and walked across toward the dugout.

It was the seventh. Now there were three innings and nine outs to go. Tension increased. Each out drew a roar, every deep fly ball a half-suppressed groan as it was hit, a mighty shout as it was caught. Throughout the park, the crowd played scoreboard when the Cards picked up a run, then another, with the Braves ahead, 6-3. A kid in the first-base stands put the hex on Philadelphia. He drew his right hand across his forehead, touched his right thumb with his left thumb, and held them that way all through the inning.

The hex worked. The second hitter got a pass, but again a lightning double play took Speedy out of it.

The crowd was for him; the Dodger bench was back of him every minute—nobody more so than the Schoolboy, who began to understand and appreciate the strain growing with every inning. It made him realize the test of character the man was enduring. His teammates let him entirely alone as he slumped to the bench between innings, opening up a wide space for him to stretch out where the Doc could work on his arm, now reddish from the constant rubbing.

Does he know he has a no-hitter going for him? thought Schoolie. Of course; he's been round too long not to know. Ask him ten years from today, and he'll tell you every single pitch he threw to each batter; that is, if he makes it.

This is an added strain, one more thing to wear him down beside that absolute necessity of holding off the Philly sluggers and winning the game, to stay in the race for the pennant.

In the eighth, he got two quick strikes on the first man,

who then smacked a grounder to Bobby Russell. Speedy did not watch the play; he was leaning over, busy with the rosin bag. He knew. Next he pushed the curve past the second batter for a third strike, the roaring increasing, rising, sweeping the field in a mighty volume.

Four outs to go.

The third man in the eighth stepped in. Yes, only four to go, thought Schoolie, and don't I know how he feels— how weary he is, not only from the physical exertion, but from that constant strain coming with every man at the plate. And here's the worst one of all. The Philadelphia slugger was up again.

A called strike. An outside pitch that missed the corner by the tiniest of margins. Speedy then hit the other corner, to go ahead 1-2. He stood wiping the sweat from his forehead with that familiar gesture; and Schoolboy Johnson, leaning forward, fidgety on the bench, saw plainly enough what the veteran was enduring; suffered with him, strained every second and on each pitch.

He wasted a ball, close. Nobody was digging in on him; if they did, he'd flip them over on their rear. But at 2 and 2, the Philadelphia batter tagged it.

Schoolie rose quickly. There she goes! There goes his no-hitter, anyhow. For the first time that afternoon it was a well-hit ball, and to the Schoolboy even the sound of the bat was different. At first it seemed to be headed over the fence. Then, he realized it didn't have the legs, but was a screaming drive toward the boards in right for extra bases.

Karl Case, head down, back to the plate, tore for the wall. As he hit the cinders he dug in, whirled around, leaped up against the wall, his glove in the air.

The ball disappeared from sight.

Did he nab it? No, he missed it. He got it? Nobody could tell.

Karl tumbled to the ground, picked himself up, and came trotting in. The shrieking and shouting from the bleachers in deep right told the story. Karl had the ball in his glove.

At last, the top of the ninth. The lower part of the Phils' batting order was due up; yet this was the toughest part of all. Speedy tossed in his warm-ups, Sunny Jim fairly dancing behind the plate, chucking the ball back hard and straight into his glove.

At last he was ready. Watch yourself, man. Watch your control. Remember what the book says on every hitter. This boy has been known to tee off unexpectedly on a high, inside one. Keep it low. One mistake, and you're gone. A second's relaxation, a little carelessness, and you've lost your no-hitter. Or, again, luck may leave you. A blooper can fall in. An accidental hit off the end of a bat can dribble down the line untouched. Yes, this is the hardest of all.

Everyone was up now. They yelled and shouted, then quiet covered the ball park as he took his windup, and a mighty roar went up as he threw in the strike. Tight with emotion, tense with the fatigue of watching, sitting there unable to do anything, the Schoolie hardly dared look. Speedy's pitch was a beauty, across the letters. Then a close one, low and near the hitter, who jumped back. It was the veteran's trick, a pitch to tell the batter off, to say: You think I'm bushed? Wrong, feller. I've still got it.

Then came a high, towering foul. From the moment it was hit, the pitcher knew it was out of play; he wasted no time watching it, although Highpockets raced toward the stands. Speedy took a new ball from the catcher, wound up carefully, but missed the plate for the second ball.

Then he tossed in his change-up. The batter swung round completely. The stands cheered with delight, stamping their feet, waving at him. Everyone was watching, hoping, as a pinch hitter came to the plate.

Sunny Jim came out to the mound, slowly. Speedy nodded calmly, patted the squat catcher on the back, the coolest person in the park. Yet inwardly, as the Schoolboy well knew, he must be a furnace. That's real control, that is.

The pitcher turned toward the plate and went to work. The batter bunted the first pitch, a beautiful hobbled bunt along the grass by the third-base line. But the old pro was ready. He ran over, scooped it up, and fired a strike to Red.

Only one man left, thought Schoolie. Hope he makes it.

He must make it; he deserves to make it—nineteen years in the majors and never tossed a no-hitter. Now he's three strikes away. Only one man left; that was the thought of every human being in the stands.

Only one man to go, Speedy Mason repeated to himself on the mound. But he used the phrase differently. I'm bushed. I've only got one batter left in me. I can handle one man, this man; then I'm through.

He took his time. He leaned over and fingered the rosin bag, wiped his forehead with his sleeve, replaced his cap, slapped his moist palm across his shirt front, glanced at the bull-pen occupants sitting quietly in right. At last, taking the sign from the catcher, he stood there. The late September sun was dropping behind the stands; almost the entire diamond was in shadow. The ball was hard to see now; he knew he had this riding for him.

And I need it, too, he thought.

Another pinch hitter stepped in. Speedy got the strike with a slider, and the crowd went wild. He wasted the next one. Silence over the stands. Even the chatter around the diamond died away. No use giving this guy the old pepper. He knows his stuff, thought the boys. And every one of the eight men was feeling the same thing. Only one to go. Hope the ball doesn't come my way. If it does, just play it like another out in any other game.

Then he burned it in and caught the batter looking. The whole ball park was in a frenzy, the fans yelling, cheering, appealing for another strike. One strike away from a no-hitter.

He didn't need to save anything now. What little was left he could use. It's now or never. He reared back, poised a second, and blistered in the ball.

The hand of the umpire went up and Speedy Mason was surrounded. Sunny Jim reached him first. Then Red and Roy and Bobby Russell. Next, the whole Dodger bench reached the mound. Schoolboy Johnson was in the forefront of that knot of players embracing the veteran.

CHAPTER 19

That-There Russell

"Spike, he's ready," said Fat Stuff, the pitching coach. "I tell you, he's as good now as he always thought he was."

"He's got that change-up at last; he's ready, Spike," said Sunny Jim.

"Definitely, he's ready," said Speedy, who had been working with the Schoolboy every day. But the fans disagreed.

"That-there Spike Russell, he's lost his head. He's nuts, completely nuts."

"Whassermatter, wants to lose the pennant, does he?"

"Say, can you tie that? Using a kid in the most important game of the year, the whole pennant hanging on nine innings and he throws in a youngster six weeks from the bush leagues."

"Yeah, but then again he needs a pitcher, what can he do? Crayton and Mason are bushed; he's worked 'em to death. Mitchell never could beat the Phils. What can he do? He needs a pitcher."

"Aw, he ought to have his head examined, that Spike Russell, that's what."

The comment rose all over Brooklyn on the last day of the season, with the Braves and Dodgers even in the won-and-lost column, as news came through that Spike was using Schoolboy Johnson in the last game of all. Every elevator operator in the five boroughs had the same verdict.

"Say, what for he wants to chuck in Johnson?"

"Why'n he throw the game and be done with it?"

"Can you tie that one?"

"Hey, Mac, get this. Tossing that kid in, with the pennant up for grabs."

Out in a ranch house on Long Island, a girl sat at one end of a table drinking coffee and listening to the early-morning news. Finally the man behind the desk on the television screen came to the part she wanted to hear. She leaned forward attentively. The telephone rang. She went over, took the receiver off the hook, placing it carefully on the stand, still listening.

"Another clear, sunny day in the metropolitan area, much like yesterday, with the high temperature in the upper seventies. A good day for the game which may decide the National League pennant this year. At one-thirty the Dodgers will meet Philadelphia, while the Braves play Chicago in Milwaukee. The two teams are tied with ninety-two games won and sixty-one lost. Spike Russell has not yet decided upon his starter, but there is a basis for believing he will go with his young fireballer, School-boy Johnson. You recall, perhaps, that Johnson was beaned about three weeks ago in a game with Chicago, and spent almost a week in the hospital before he was released. Since then he has thrown well in the relief jobs given him, and in a four-inning stint the other day, but he has yet to finish a complete contest. The Dodgers are at full strength for this afternoon's game; but the Phillies' left-hander, Lee Krause, has a bad back and will not be available. . . ."

A door opened on the other side of the room, and a man in pajamas with a cotton bathrobe wrapped around him stood there, yawning. His bare feet were stuck in slippers and he was rather a ludicrous sight as he raised his hand to his mouth, still yawning.

"Daddy!" There was annoyance in her voice, and also real concern. "Daddy, what made you get up so early? Last night you promised you'd sleep until I woke you."

He sauntered across the room and sat down at the table as she poured some coffee for him, still yawning and stretching. "I dunno what it is, the day we hafta grab the nine-thirty plane for the West, I can't drag myself out of bed. This morning I simply couldn't sleep. I kept replaying that game all night, every ball, every pitch he made, every inning. . . ."

"Wasn't it wonderful!"

"I'll say. They claim he only threw a hundred and

eighteen pitches. Mitchell phoned last night and told me his wife bawled him out when he got home. 'What's the matter?' she asked. 'Speedy Mason is an old man and he pitches a no-hitter. You're only twenty-six. What's the matter with you?' "

"Speedy must be happy."

"He is; he'll be happier tonight if we cut him a big, juicy slice of that Series melon. There's a lot riding out there this afternoon."

"There certainly is. Here's the cream. I'll get your bacon and eggs in a minute. Guess who's pitching today."

"Mitchell. Who else has he got? Can't go with anyone else; can't get any more out of Speedy and Josh; he's just about used up all the mileage in them."

"Nope, not Mitchell."

"No? One of the bull-pen boys then. Well, maybe...."
He kept yawning.

"No, again. Johnson!"

His chair scraped on the floor. He straightened up and looked at her hard. The yawning stopped, for he was wide awake now.

"No! That right? You sure?"

"Monty Morgan said so on the eight o'clock news."

"Well, I'll be darned." He drummed the table, thinking. "Schoolboy Johnson? Well, I dunno but what that might be a smart move after all. Schoolie pitched well the other day. He could throw him in and stop them for a few innings. It's bad out in the afternoon in that light

now, and his fast ball will take off. Besides what has
Spike got left. . . . I say, who else has Spike got?"

He turned, looked around. He was alone. She had gone
out to the kitchen.

Several minutes later she came in with a tray, bearing
coffee, two eggs and enough bacon for an army, a heap
of toast. She spread this out before him.

"I was just saying, he really hasn't anyone else." He
looked at her quickly. "Most likely you'll be out there this
afternoon?"

"Wouldn't miss it for anything," she answered, her eyes
dancing.

He noticed her expression, turned to his breakfast, but-
tered some toast and attacked the eggs. "What you see in
him I can't imagine. He's a spoiled kid, or he was until
that accident. Fat Stuff says the beaning knocked some
sense into him; I'll believe it when I see it. After all, he
leaves you in a restaurant miles away from any place, then
he writes you a note of apology, and you accept it. Why
you want to come out and watch him pitch. . . ."

She patted his head. "I'm a National Leaguer, I was
brought up a National Leaguer, I want to see which team
wins the National League pennant. Besides, I'm really
coming to watch the third baseman of the Dodgers, my
favorite ballplayer. Y'know, Dad, you get to watching a
man play, you almost feel you know him after a while."

"Yeah, sure. I can't reason out what you see in this
Johnson."

"Reason? Reason? 'I have no other but a woman's reason: I think him so, because I think him so.' Get it, Dad?"

"Sure. Sometimes I wish I'd sent you to college; you'd have got your fill of books, you wouldn't always be reading poetry and throwing it at me."

"No, and I probably wouldn't be working as a window designer for a hundred and a quarter a week, either."

"Frankly, Maxine, I don't get it. This clod walks out on you . . . leaves you flat in a restaurant. . . ."

"He had provocation."

"He had what?"

"He'd made a fool of himself before forty thousand fans, he was sore all over. Can't you put yourself in his place a second? So naturally, when I told him off. . . ."

"Ha, you told him off? What did you say?"

"Why, I suggested he was acting like a child and he should grow up, that his mistakes were all his own fault, that. . . ."

"So then he got mad and walked out. Yet you still want to watch him pitch. I don't get it." He shook his head, his mouth full of toast. "No, I . . . simply . . . don't . . . get it."

"Look, Dad, I want to see this game, I want to see *you* play, I want to see the Dodgers win. Here's one I wouldn't miss, not if it cost me my job. If Schoolboy does pitch, I'll be interested; why not? And if he goes in there, I bet you he'll be different. . . ."

"He'd better be, if we're to win the pennant."

"He will be, he's changed, Fat Stuff says so. I just know he is. You watch, you'll see for yourself this afternoon."

"Hope you're right. My guess is he'll last four innings, blow up, and paste Stubblebeard in the jaw over a strike decision. By the way, I could eat some more eggs."

CHAPTER 20

The Girl in Box 56

"Here ya are, get your score card . . . can't tell the players without a score card . . . get your score card, folks. . . ."

The fans had been standing in line for hours during the cool September night, ever since the game of the previous afternoon, when they began forming up. They were tired now; they were weary and beaten. But they were inside the park and they were going to see the game. The big game. The game they hoped would win the National League race.

"Cool drinks . . . ice-cold drinks, folks, get your ice-cold drinks. . . ."

They perched like birds on the rafters, clinging with one hand; they stood four deep behind the stands; they peered on tiptoes over the shoulder of the fat man in front; they roosted dangerously on the iron railings watching as best they could, leaning around a pillar to see the plate, twisting the other way as a hard-hit ball in batting practice fell into the center-field stands, sitting out in the distant bleachers, high up in the second tier under the roof, portables glued to their ears to catch the returns from Milwaukee before they were flashed on the scoreboard.

Down in a box just back of the playing field, a man in the front row leaned out toward the Dodger bench. Then he turned to his companion. "Hey, see that! There's Mason and the Schoolboy together on the bench like a couple of pals. Get that! I always thought they hated each other's guts."

A girl sitting in the next box caught these words. She, too, glanced across, her heart beating a little faster as she saw the pair on the long bench in the shade. The Schoolboy was stern, bending forward with set lips, plainly feeling the responsibility upon him, nodding ever so slightly at Speedy's earnest injunctions.

They're friends now, she thought; they've made it up, he's got some sense hammered into him at last. He's changed, I'm sure he's changed, he simply must be changed, or Spike Russell wouldn't go with him this afternoon. I'll be proud of him today.

On the bench the old pitcher gripped the boy's shoulder as if he meant what he was saying. He did. "You can do it, Schoolie, you got the stuff; you're a fine pitcher, and don't forget it a single minute. Just keep that ball between the belt and the knees, and they aren't going to hit you to amount to anything. Remember, Burke is their only low-ball hitter; be sure and pitch him high and tight.

And whatever happens, use that change-up; you've learned it, use it in the pinches. . . ."

A roar swept the field. The Dodgers leaped from the bench, eager to get into action.

One final slap on the back. "I believe in you. You can do it, kid."

From the front row of Box 56, she watched him walk out to the mound, the burden of baseball history on those broad shoulders, ten thousand dollars for each man riding on his control, on almost every pitch and every move he made—or didn't make.

The preliminaries over, Schoolboy Johnson wound up and let go. The hand of the umpire fairly leaped into the air. Strike one!

It was a good sign; the crowd cheered with approval. They yelled at the second pitch, a fast ball cutting the plate as a knife cuts cheese. This, too, was a sign that the big boy had it. The fans looked at each other, nodding.

"Say . . . mebbe that Spike Russell was smart after all, Mac. D'ja see that speed?"

In Box 56, the girl in the front row relaxed a little as she heard the words of approbation around her. This is the day. He's really got it at last. I'm going to be proud of him this afternoon.

Strike three!

The Philadelphia batter went back to the bench, but there was confidence in his remark as he sat down among his teammates. "Fast? Sure he's fast, he's always fast at the start of a game. Why, you can't see the ball for the smoke on it. Wait till the fifth or sixth; we'll get to him all right."

Nobody scored in the opening three innings. The Schoolboy struck out two in the first and the last two in the second; got Burke, the Phils' slugger, to ground out in that inning as the crowd cheered. Let's see, five strikeouts in three innings; he sure is tough today. Spike Russell was mebbe right after all. . . .

All the time and every minute the Phils' coaches and the bench jockeys were on him.

"Hey there, puddin'head. . . ."

"Say, Schoolboy, learned to read yet?"

"How's your pal, George Morris?"

And in return the Dodger infield tried to drown them out with their chatter, supporting him every minute.

"Attaboy, Schoolie, attaboy. . . ."

"Put it in the hole in his head, Schoolboy. . . ."

Suddenly the next batter connected. He caught the fast ball as they had all been trying to do, laced it to deep left center, between Jackson and Highpockets. The two fastest men on the team chased it, but the runner was sliding under the tag as the ball reached Roy Tucker standing over third.

"What happened? What happened? Did he score?" asked the standees, who could see nothing behind the rows of people in front. "What happened?"

This is it, thought the girl in Box 56. This is the pay-off; if he meets this test he's safe.

The first strike knifed the plate as the batter took it. He wiggled his bat nervously while the runner at third danced up and down the base path, and the coaches, the enemy bench, even the players far out in the visitors' bull pen yelled and shouted.

"Hey, puddin'head. . . ."

"Say, Schoolboy, you shave yet?"

"Hey, Schoolboy, George Morris sends regards."

Bang! Another strike edged the corner, a fast ball the batter didn't even offer at. One to go.

One more strike and he's safe, thought the girl; one strike and he's come through the test. And I'll be proud. She watched him, motionless on the mound, one eye on that dancing figure between third and the plate.

It's risky, he said to himself as he poised motionless astride the rubber. It's a gamble, it's risky with everything riding on one pitch; but I have to do it. I have to prove to myself I can do it.

He shook off his catcher, and came in with the change-up. The batter swung a foot ahead of the ball, and Sunny Jim rolled it exultantly out toward the box and turned away.

Meanwhile Milwaukee was o-o in the second. Here and there in the crowded stands, and especially among the mob packed five deep at the rear of the center section, the fans had radios at their ears. Karl Case stepped in and belted a fast ball for two bases and, after Red Allen flied out, he scored on Roy Tucker's smartly placed single over third. At last there was a margin to work on.

The fifth started well too. The Schoolboy got the first two hitters—one on a pop-up to Ed Peters, and the next on a strike-out. The girl in the front box noticed that he was burning in his first pitch on every batter. That was a good sign.

But with two down, he gave up his first base on balls, and on the hit and run, the next batter shot a drive to right which fell in safely. Karl charged it; but the man on first, off with the pitch, got all the way around to third.

Now there was action in the Dodger bull pen for the first time.

"Slow down, slow down . . . take yer time, Schoolie . . . take yer time!" shouted Speedy Mason from the bench, through cupped hands. Over all that noise, over the yells and the jeers coming out of the visitors' dugout and from the coaching lines, the familiar tone of the veteran pitcher came strong and clear. It reassured the Schoolboy, settled him down, gave him strength and confidence.

So he took plenty of time, leaning over and fiddling with the rosin bag. He wiped his forehead with his sleeve, hitched at his belt, looked over toward first, took the sign from Sunny Jim, nodded, blew into his glove mechanically.

The voice of the umpire at third broke in. "Lemme see that ball."

He turned, annoyed. Look, I'm not throwing spitters; I'm good, that's all. I got it today, see?

Disturbed by the break in his concentration, anxious to start pitching again, he turned and, without thinking, rolled the ball briskly toward third base, where the man in blue stood back of the bag.

The ball rolled past; the umpire standing there made no move to intercept it.

But the runner moved—and fast. As he dashed for the plate, Roy Tucker raced for the ball and threw home, too late to catch him sliding in. Now the score was tied. And there was a man on second.

The stands hummed and buzzed in excitement. At first everyone was puzzled, and rows of standees at the back pleaded for information.

"What happened? What happened?"

Schoolie, flushed and irritated, strode toward third, realizing that he had fallen for the oldest of all tricks in the game except the hidden-ball gag. That order had not been given by the umpire, but by the Philly runner on third base.

The crowd got it now; they roared with dismay as he stood chin to chin with the umpire, protesting.

"Look here, Stubble, you can't do that to me! I called time, you can't do that. . . ."

The umpire waved him off. "You called nothing—and you know it. Play ball!"

The Schoolboy stood shaking his head, arguing, talking

loudly, Roy and Ed Peters beside him. The longer he stood, the greater the roar from the stands, the wilder the noises from the Philadelphia bench. And the more angry he became.

The bench jockeys were after him. Towels came out of their dugout, sailed through the air, and fell before the steps.

Oh-oh, this is bad, thought the girl in Box 56. This is really bad. Get in there and pitch, quick. He's up against it now, up against himself, really against himself again.

Peering out from under his cap in the Dodger dugout, Speedy watched intently, feeling the same thing. This is brutal. Stop talking, kid, quit horsing around, get in there and throw that ball. Forget what's happened. Or else you're finished, brother—not just for this game but for major-league ball.

Finally Schoolboy walked slowly back to the mound, shaking his head and talking to himself.

Shoot, that old Stubblebeard, that Stubble always did have it in for me. He was glad when George Morris spiked me; he called my best pitches wide and cost me that game in Chicago. Always he gives me the wrong end of the stick, always. That Stubblebeard! How can a man beat a whole team and the umpire too—that's what I'd like to know.

He toed the rubber, glanced back at second where the runner was dancing off the bag, and quickly, with no windup, threw.

Sunny Jim, his glove high in the air, jumped. So did the man off second.

For the pitch was ten feet above the catcher's mitt. The squat little man tossed off his mask as he turned and took after the ball, now bouncing back beside the stands. It was a race between catcher and runner for that vital extra run.

Schoolie came in to cover, but the man slid in between his legs before Sunny Jim burned the ball to the plate. And the Dodgers were behind, 1-2.

A vast roar rose over the stands, over the whole field. Suddenly another, a peculiarly different and even louder noise swept the park. The figure 3 was falling into Milwaukee's third-inning slot on the scoreboard.

The girl in Box 56 hardly heard the noise. For she was thinking about that disconsolate figure walking back to the plate. He really hasn't changed, has he? He seemed so sure of himself, so confident, so self-reliant, and yet he's completely gone to pieces now. I hoped so much for him, wanted so much for him. I was sure he had licked his disposition. I was going to be so proud of him, too.

All around, she heard the comments of the fans.

"That Johnson. . . ."

"What can you expect?"

"Russell's crazy, chucking away the pennant. Why don't he get him out of there before it's too late!"

All around, everyone made the same remarks. Then she looked carefully along the bench until she saw the familiar figure of Spike Russell, at the far end of the dug-out.

A man beside him—one of the coaches, obviously—had a telephone at his ear. "Ask Fatso is Mitchell ready."

They watched with attention as the Schoolboy turned and slumped back to the box, disaster in his bearing, discouragement even in the set of his head and shoulders.

"Says Mitchell is all ready, set to go," said the coach.

"Good. Have him quit throwing. If Schoolie loses this man, he's out."

The next batter was Burke, the Philadelphia long-ball hitter.

CHAPTER 21

Strikeouts: Johnson, 11

All round the field the fans watched with dismay.

"There ya are. He's blowing wide open. Whad' I tell ya?"

"That-there Schoolie can't take it, never could."

"Russell oughta have his head examined, leaving him in there."

Sunny Jim trundled back to the plate, yelled at Schoolie for the ball, and stood examining it attentively. He tossed it back to the man in blue. Quite obviously he was stalling for time; nevertheless, the umpire looked the ball over and handed him another. Sunny Jim burned it across the diamond to Bobby at second, who flipped it backhanded to Ed Peters, who threw in turn to Roy at third.

Rubbing it with care, Roy Tucker walked slowly across the diamond toward the mound, extending the ball to the Schoolboy, who stepped from the mound to meet him.

The veteran handed it over, and the sentence he uttered hit the pitcher with the force of a crack on the jaw.

"Listen, you dope, quit it."

Schoolie stared at him. "Wha . . . at?"

"Quit it. You hear me?"

"Quit what?"

"Quit being sorry for yourself. Act your age. Get in there and pitch the way you know how to."

A friendly slap on the back—the reverse of those bitter words—and the veteran turned away, leaving Schoolie with the ball tucked in his fist, looking after him. For a few seconds he stood motionless. To the thousands in the stands this incident was a vote of approval from the old third baseman, and the young pitcher was merely pulling himself up after the shock of that wild pitch and the ensuing run.

But those blunt, harsh words had their effect. He suddenly recalled Speedy Mason, at his bedside in the hospital.

"Baseball is a test of character, how you react under pressure."

So he turned slowly, went for the rosin bag, as the crowd sat watching silently, almost everyone expecting a gopher ball, or some other pitch that would lose the game.

Yep, he thought, this is a test. It's a test of me. I wish to heaven I was in the showers. I wish I was at Jones Beach. I wish I was anywhere but out here with all these folks watching. But I'm not in the showers. If I've got anything at all, here's the time to show it.

The batter stood menacingly at the plate, waggling his bat as if he meant business. Sunny Jim gave the sign for the change-up, but Schoolie shook him off and threw in his fast ball. The hitter connected, a screaming drive to right, headed for the fences, deep and long.

There it goes. There's your ball game. There's the pennant, riding out of the park. . . . "Oh . . . oh . . . oh . . ." roared the crowd. "Oh . . . oh . . . oh . . . ah . . . ah . . . ah. . . ."

The liner, rising in flight, was foul by two feet.

"Ah . . . ah . . . ah. . . ." The murmur echoed all over the stands as the fans turned to each other.

"Why'n he take him out? He's blown higher'n a kite."

"Whassermatter with Russell? Must have lost his mind!"

On the mound, Schoolie took the new ball. Suddenly he remembered something that the wild pitch and the run had driven from his mind. This is Burke. High and tight to Burke. Of course; I was excited, I forgot. I paid no attention. I threw him *his* pitch, not mine.

Sunny Jim gave the sign, and this time he came in exactly where he wanted to, close to the batter's fists, right across the letters. The man spun round, the bat flying from his hands.

From third came Roy Tucker's steady voice. "Take yer time, Schoolie, take yer time and fire the horsehide offa that ball."

Once again, he stood motionless on the mound. He was cool now, in possession of himself, he knew what to do and was doing it. Jim ordered him to waste a pitch, and he obeyed. Then the catcher called for his change-up.

He was afraid, and wanted to shake him off, because he wasn't sure of that pitch. He felt more confident of his fast ball. Then he thought, No, I better do what he says. I better go all out. If I've got anything, here's the time to show it. The place to throw in a change-up is when they don't expect it.

So, nodding, he wound up and threw the ball as directed, the change-up so well concealed that the batter swung viciously in front of it. In four pitches the side was retired.

They swarmed back to the bench, Roy Tucker slapping his back, the boys calling to him down the bench as the Doc went to work on his arm.

"Attaboy, Schoolboy."

"Tha's chucking, Schoolie."

"Now let's go get him some runs."

Get him some runs they did. This was a gutsy team, a worn and ancient team, but one that responded to challenges. It was in their make-up, they were accustomed to fighting from behind, they knew how to put out a little bit extra. A single by Bobby Russell, a sacrifice, and a poke into the stands by Highpockets, and the score was 3-2, the Dodgers again in the lead.

Schoolie got his ninth strike-out in the top of the sixth.

His fast ball was taking off now, his control perfect; he had lost every trace of nerves, and dominated the diamond. He wasn't overpowering the hitters; but his fast one was hopping, and he could put it just where he wanted. Following every sign with attention, he didn't let a single batter reach first. Even the chatter and the insults from the opposing bench subsided.

The seventh was uneventful except for one thing. It was the first inning in which the Schoolboy didn't strike anyone out. By this time it was the fifth in Milwaukee, the Cubs had picked up a couple of runs, and there was an identical count—the Braves leading, 3-2. The pennant was still up for grabs.

The first batter in the top of the eighth mistimed a change-up and the ball bounced high, midway to the pitcher's box. Schoolie stood waiting for it to come down. He burned the throw to first, but the delay had been sufficient for the runner to beat the ball to the bag. This was the first man aboard since the fifth inning.

Attentively, and with care, he worked on the next hitter, putting the ball just where he wanted to, low and around the knees. On the 2-2 count, the batter smacked a brisk grounder, a double-play ball right at Roy Tucker back of third.

The old third baseman came in, stooped over, went down for the routine chance, but the ball wasn't there. For no reason it rolled between his legs onto the outfield grass, and before Ed Peters, backing up, could retrieve it, there were runners on first and third.

More action in the Dodger bull pen. The Phils' bench came alive with shouts and insults again.

Sunny Jim waddled to the mound. Roy walked over toward them, touching the Schoolboy on the arm.

"That's the worst, Schoolie, the worst ever. I'm sorry, way you're throwing, to do a thing like that."

He spun round. "Forget it, Roy, just forget it. We'll get the next one." He patted the third baseman's back and stepped to the mound.

Just then a sudden outburst of noise all over the park upset his concentration. A glance at the scoreboard showed the Cubs had scored two runs and were leading the Braves, 4-3.

He took off his cap, the rim soaking with sweat, and slapped it twice on his thigh. He punched the ball from glove to hand, from hand to glove, as Sunny Jim, mask in one fist, returned to the plate. Bad luck? Yep, but forget it. Tough? Sure, but that's baseball. Go to work on the batter.

Watching the dancing runner off third, he threw in his fast ball. The batter was waiting and ready. He slashed at it and connected, a furious, screaming, low liner toward third. Roy had been holding the bag, coming in from the grass for a possible squeeze play, and the ball came like a rifle shot at his feet. It seemed sure to go through.

Somehow, he knocked it down as it hit the dirt, the force of the blow almost bowling him over. He scrambled for it, straightened up, feinted toward the plate. The man dove back, so Roy whirled and threw hard to Bobby Russell, who tagged the sliding runner, and shot the ball to Red on first.

It was a double play.

The crowd cheered, the crowd shouted; they yelled their delight, they roared from every corner of the stands. Then a curious thing happened. Red Allen turned, rolled the ball gently toward the plate, and walked over in the direction of the bench, tossing aside his glove.

The alert base runner on third instantly grasped the situation. Red, in his tightness, had forgot that this was only the second out. There was the ball, bobbling along the grass close to the foul line with nobody near it, so he lit out at full speed for the plate.

Sunny Jim had to cover home, while Schoolie, on the mound, stood open-mouthed, completely upset, too stunned even to try for the ball. There was no play; the runner scored, standing up, to tie the score again, at 3-3.

The whole Philadelphia bench rose and came out, laughing and jeering. They slapped and pounded the quick-thinking base runner, they yelled at Schoolie standing disconsolately on the rubber, they roared with delight at this break which had given them an unexpected run. A murmur of disappointment swept the field as Red, crimson with chagrin, walked slowly out.

At first Schoolie turned away and leaned over the rosin bag. First Roy, then Red! What do you have to do to win? Are these guys with me or against me? A scratch hit, an error, and an attack of amnesia, and the score is tied. Momentarily he became the Schoolie of old, sore and bitter all over.

But as they gathered around—Sunny Jim and Ed Peters; Roy and Bobby Russell; Red, speechless with disgust at himself—the Schoolboy pulled himself together. After those seconds of anger and annoyance, he was the coolest of them all.

"O.K., fellers, leave this to me. Leave this man to me."

As they went slowly back to their places, every man thought the same thing. He'll crack now, for sure. He'll bust wide open. From under their caps they peered anxiously toward the dugout to see what Spike would do.

This is it, here we go, everyone thought. Only one person watching had confidence in Schoolboy Johnson—the girl in Box 56.

It was over so quickly—and so painlessly. The curve that edged the plate and sent the hand of the umpire into the air. The change-up that caught the batter looking. And the fast ball on which he swung helplessly. The side was out and the inning was over.

Now Schoolboy Johnson had struck out ten batters.

Sunny Jim, first to bat in the eighth, lined a single to right. The crowd watched silently, wondering whether a pinch hitter would come up, but Spike stayed with his pitcher as he had all afternoon. On the second ball, the Schoolboy dropped a perfect bunt that advanced Sunny Jim to second. Bobby Russell struck out. Then Roy Tucker, the toughest money player in the business, plastered a long single against the boards in right, and the little catcher, fast for a fat man, scampered home with the tie-breaking run. The Dodgers now led, 4-3.

It was the first of the ninth. After the warm-ups, Sunny Jim waddled out to the mound and handed Schoolie the baseball.

"Get the first one, son. That's the big man." Back he went, squatting down behind the plate.

Now the Schoolboy bore down with everything he had. There he stood, hands on his hips, watching as the Phils' pinch hitter smacked a soaring fly ball that Karl Case smothered without taking six steps. Then came another pinch hitter, who grounded to Ed Peters at short. Ed fairly hurled himself at the ball and fired a careful strike to Red at first.

The crowd went wild. What a pitcher! Is that guy fast! He's really got it today. A great hurler, this kid, everyone agreed.

Indeed the Schoolboy was the master now. He was on top of every man who faced him. They came up and he disposed of each one, making him do what he wanted. He finished with a blinding burst of speed, throwing in three quick pitches as though he was tired of the game, bored by it all, anxious to get into the showers.

Roy Tucker, with two leaps, was the first one to reach him. Speedy Mason, from the bench, was right on his heels.

CHAPTER 22

Clubhouse Celebration

Arms upraised in triumph, the Schoolboy leaped from the mound into the outstretched arms of Speedy Mason and Roy.

Sunny Jim, racing out from the plate with his mask still on and the ball tight in his fist, joined the embrace. Instantly there was a struggling knot about him: the veterans and the youngsters, the men who had fought uphill all summer and come back to win by a single game; Ed Peters and Red Allen; Bobby Russell, followed by the outfielders, Karl and Highpockets and Jackson Jones.

They kissed him, they slapped his back, his arms, his shoulders, any part of him they could reach. Swirling, twisting, yet staying together as they had all season, this group of sweating, happy ballplayers reached the dugout, the passage under the stands.

"Yippee . . . yea. . . ."

"Boy . . . did that one seem like five games?"

"Wowser, we won it, they said we couldn't. . . ."

Clack-clack, clackety-clack, clack-clack, clackety-clack, their spikes resounded upon the concrete ramp as they pushed through the door to the dressing room, where a uniformed attendant stood trying to hold back half of Brooklyn.

Once inside, they couldn't sit down. Flushed and excited, they walked about, hugging each other and shaking hands hilariously with MacManus, with old Chiselbeak, with the Doc, with each other. After them came the sports writers from the press box, the boys regularly assigned to the Dodgers trying to hide their delight as they cornered individuals for interviews and quotes.

Roy Tucker, the oldest, was the first to slump to a bench.

"Yeah . . . well, lemme tell you something, Casey, this club showed plenty to be down like that and come back. They hung on, they sure did hang on, and nobody could catch them in the clutch." He was impersonal, as if talking about another ball club. "What? What's that? That error? How come? I dunno. Honest, I don't really know; it was the easiest kind of a chance. See, boy, when I make a mistake it's a beaut. Imagine slipping up on a roller like that. Why, I had it, I had it in my hands, then I looked down and it wasn't there. . . ."

Seated on a trunk in one corner, Sunny Jim was talking to a couple of reporters. He held up his left hand. Three fingers were puffed and swollen.

"Fast! You ask me was he fast? Man, he sure was. He did this to my fingers in the first three innings. Yessir, he was fast all-right-all-right."

Casey joined the little group, a pencil and a folded piece of copy paper in his hands. "Maybe," he said, overhearing the last sentence. "Maybe. But your boy was lucky on that long foul of Burke's in the fifth. Couple of feet the other way, and good-by ball game. You must have called the wrong pitch that time, didn't ya, Jim?"

Sunny Jim looked up. His eyes sparkled. "Why, sure I called the wrong pitch; catcher always calls the wrong pitch when the ball goes up there in the stands. Yes, he hit it, that's for sure. We were lucky 'twas foul, as you say. But Casey, you may have noticed he never got another to belt. He smacked the low ball he liked, but Schoolie didn't let him see another. Believe me, that strikeout of Burke's was the big play, the turning point of the game. After that, if he hits one he hits our pitch, not his.

"And that last batter, the pinch hitter there, remember? Boy, he really caught that guy looking, didn't he? Why the man just stood there for the last strike. Well, the kid's one great pitcher and this is a mighty fine ball club. I'm proud to be a part of it."

Piercing yells suddenly filled the room. The Milwaukee game was over and the Braves had lost.

"Whoopee!"

"We're the champs, fellers."

"The champs, that's us."

"We came through when the chips were down," shouted Josh Crayton, parading around in shorts and shower clogs, a towel around his neck. "They said we couldn't do it, but we did."

The amateur band which had squeezed into the room, one by one, began playing "The Darktown Strutters' Ball." Someone tossed ice water over Red Allen as he went toward the showers, naked, and Highpockets took Jackson Jones's new straw hat from the top of his locker, poured Seven-Up into it, and jammed it down on the center fielder's head. Bobby Russell and Karl Case were jitterbugging, a horn was blowing in the background, and on the bench before his locker the hero of the day was surrounded by a tight circle of sports writers.

"Ya know, Schoolie, you only threw a hundred and twenty-three pitches in all?" asked one man.

"No! That correct?"

"That's right. 'Nother thing, twenty-two of the batters who faced you took the first strike."

"That I'm not surprised at. We had a hunch they'd try to wear me down, take the first one mostly, so I tried to sneak it in there."

Now the newsreel and television people swarmed in, setting up their cumbersome apparatus. Flash bulbs added to the general confusion. But the circle didn't break; the sports writers refused to give ground. They kept tight about Schoolboy Johnson; he was their captive and they intended to get their job done first. So the camera men climbed onto chairs, shouting down to where he sat on the low bench.

"That error of Tucker's in the eighth, the grounder he let through, that bother you much?" asked a reporter.

He bristled. His head came up quickly and he looked his questioner in the eye. His voice was tired, taut, edgy; yet there was an undertone of happy excitement in it, too.

"Brother, any man's done as much as Roy Tucker to win this pennant for us, why, he's entitled to boot one now and then. That error, lemme tell ya something, it put the iron into me, made me bear down all the harder. Roy Tucker is one grand ballplayer; believe me, he's a man to have on your side. So is that catcher of ours, and all the rest, the best gang I ever played with."

The circle broke as the camera men finally elbowed their way inside, pulling Spike Russell with them. He stood beside the bench, one arm over his young pitcher's shoulder, a grin on his weary, lined face.

"Shake hands, Spike . . . shake hands, please . . . shake hands with him. That's right. Again . . . look over here . . . look this way . . . look up here, up here, please. . . ."

They took pictures endlessly, until a thought came to Schoolboy Johnson. The most important person of all was missing.

"Hey! Where's Speedy? Take me with Speedy Mason, fellers. The credit's all his. If I'm a pitcher, he's the man who made me."

He jumped up, stood on the bench, and looked around

the smoky, packed room. Speedy Mason had showered and was sitting before his locker in shorts, with a towel around his neck. He was leaning over, a cigarette in his mouth, as exhausted as if he had pitched that afternoon himself.

Schoolie leaped down and pushed through the circle. The group dissolved and trailed him across the room, where it formed again around the two men. Now the photographers were at work once more, taking the wise old pitcher who had reached the place where the end was in sight, and the youngster who had only begun the long climb to the heights. They snapped them shaking hands, they took them laughing and grinning, with Schoolie's arm affectionately around Speedy's shoulder, and in many other poses. The flash bulbs flared and the cameras clicked.

"Speedy taught me that change-up, Casey; there's where I got it. That was the pitch I used to strike out Burke in the fifth. It was Speedy taught it to me, and it sure came in handy this afternoon."

Casey, in the front row of the circle, kept scribbling. Then he felt someone shove his left elbow from behind. The newsreel and television men had been pushing, shoving, ever since they entered the room, so he planted his feet apart and stood firm. A second or two later he saw who it was. Johnny O'Brien, the bat boy, was trying hard to get inside that circle.

He pushed, edged one man, was thrust back, tried another opening and failed. All the while the Schoolboy, inside the circle, was talking and laughing. Casey watched the lad.

Now what on earth is biting that kid, he wondered.

Finally he saw him get down on his hands and knees. Headfirst he squeezed through two pairs of legs and into the circle. Then he scrambled to his feet and leaned over the Schoolboy, as the photographers yelled at him to move away.

"There's a lady waiting for you in Box 56. She said you wasn't to hurry, Schoolie."